D1600670

ANTHONY RYAN

This special signed edition is limited to
1000 numbered copies and 26 lettered copies.

This is copy 766 .

Across the Sorrow Sea

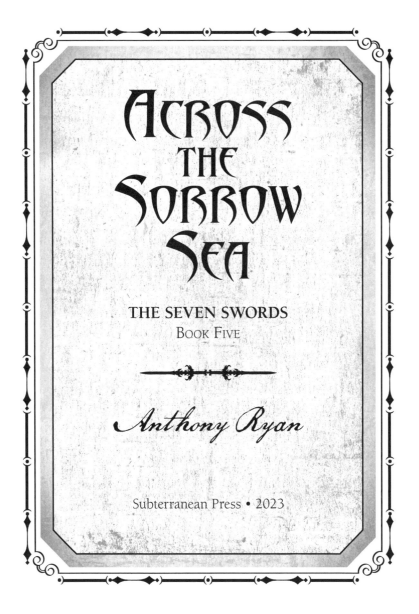

ACROSS THE SORROW SEA

THE SEVEN SWORDS
BOOK FIVE

Anthony Ryan

Subterranean Press • 2023

First Edition

ISBN
978-1-64524-155-3

Subterranean Press
PO Box 190106
Burton, MI 48519

subterraneanpress.com

Manufactured in the United States of America

To the masters of maritime adventure
and seafaring fantasy: Douglas Reeman,
CS Forester, and Robin Hobb.

Neither storm nor the wide and perilous sea
Can bar the truly righteous from the gift of truth
—*Injunctions of the First Risen.*

Chapter One

THE DEMON'S TALE

•)———(•)———(•

*T*ime is supposed to succour a longing for the sight of old haunts, Lakorath opined in an acerbic drawl. *And yet, I find my desire never to behold this grey misery again to be undimmed.*

Guyime had to admit that the unceasing, slate-hued swell beneath a perennially overcast sky made an ominous and unwelcoming vista. The deck of the *Atheria's Grace* was constantly damp from the unremitting drizzle and he couldn't recall glimpsing blue sky or unclouded sun for days now.

Despite the unnatural scale of his years, he had scant experience of the vast body of water known in Valkerin as the *Axuntus Nuarem*, or the Fifth Sea in most modern tongues. It was notorious as the most fractious and perilous of all the five seas. Riven with storms at all seasons, it was also home to the most vicious breeds of shark and, more dangerous still, pirates of inordinate number and merciless reputation. Despite its troubled tides, the Fifth Sea remained a valuable trade route. Caravans bearing all manner of desirable goods from the enigmatic lands of the Kalthar Imperium terminated their epic journeys at the ports on its eastern shore. From there, they were shipped to the hungry merchants of the

other four seas, thereby providing the pirates with an unending supply of rich pickings. The captain of the *Atheria's Grace*
had assured Orsena that their course was too far west to attract
unwanted attention, though Guyime noted the way the fellow's
lively gaze flicked over the horizon with agitated constancy.

"Coming here was your idea," he reminded the demon,
a small grin curling the corners of his mouth as he felt the
annoyed thrum of the sword on his back.

In service to your mad enterprise, Lakorath replied. *In which
I am compelled to partake through no agency of my own.* He let out
a thin sigh of tolerated indignity. *What a trial it is to be a slave to
mortals.*

"If what you say is true, mayhap our mutual bondage will
soon be at an end."

A thin, grudging chuckle, laden with disparagement. *Is any
course we ever tread that easy, my liege?*

To this, Guyime could only grunt in soft acknowledgement.
From the Execration to the Northern Kingdom, their journey
had been one of recurrent danger, not to mention frequent
destruction for those unfortunate souls who lay in their path.
Still, he entertained no thought of turning aside. Ever since the
Mad God first spoke of the Seven Swords, he had known this
would be his mission, even should it cost him his life.

Perhaps that's the point, Lakorath suggested, ever keen to
explore the darker corners of Guyime's thoughts. *After centuries
of trying to get yourself killed, you finally found the one method that
might actually work.*

Guyime gave no reply, unwilling to let the demon bait him.
Instead, he returned his attention to the unfurled map he held,
squinting at the line coiling across its surface. "On the move

again," he muttered, watching the line trace a slow course around the base of a mountain range he judged to be well over a thousand miles north of his current position. "Where is she going?"

Most likely, she endeavours to craft another trap, Lakorath replied. *I told you that thing would be useless now.*

"You've told me many things across the span of many years, much of which I regret listening to."

Guyime frowned as he watched the line's progress, feeling a sense of familiarity in its sluggish but inexorable course. He had never visited the region depicted on this portion of the map, a mountainous stretch of country north of the Fourth Sea that bordered the vast wasteland of the Sunless Steppes. According to every account he had ever heard, there was nothing of significance on the steppes save ancient ruins and poor soil where little grew. Ekiri, however, or rather, the demon inhabiting the Crystal Dagger she carried, clearly saw something of interest in the region. Unless Lakorath was right, as he often was, and it was simply another lure into an ambush, one perhaps even more deadly than the dire wights of Blackfyre Keep.

"Enough evasion from you, demon," he said, lowering the map. "You promised coming here would bring us closer to claiming all the Seven Swords. Now, I'll have the why of it from you."

His years of exposure to the creature in the sword had imbued an ability to read its moods, which were often easily categorised into resentment or malicious enjoyment of human woe. Now, however, the demon's thoughts were both more sombre and complex. Guyime felt Lakorath's urge to taunt him, prick his anger with more obfuscation. He expected the demon to enquire what Guyime would do should no answer be forthcoming. Cast the sword into the sea, perhaps? But there was more beneath the usual demonic malice, a sense of resignation entwined with something more, an emotion he hadn't suspected lurked in what passed for this being's heart: determination. Lakorath, it transpired, was now as committed to this mission as the cursed mortal who carried him.

Have you ever heard the name Calvius Arkelion? the demon asked.

Searching his memory, Guyime found a few scraps of knowledge. "A character of ancient myth," he said. "In the days of the Valkerin Empire, philosophers employed him as an archetypal wise man, an insightful foil for the machinations of greedy nobles or would-be tyrants."

Sometimes I forget how learned you are, my liege. Or perhaps you've just been spending too much time with that scholarly rat below.

"The tale, demon," Guyime insisted with a growl.

Calvius Arkelion was no mere myth, but a real, living man born centuries before the rise of Valkeris. As for his wisdom, well, I'll let you be the judge. Although he termed himself a philosopher, a soul intent upon dissecting the mysteries of the world and the forces that bind it, he was, in truth, a sorcerer. Perhaps the most powerful to ever live, at least in my experience, which is, as you know, extensive. For I like to flatter myself that no other mortal could have trapped me in this steel prison, though I mostly ascribe my misfortune to my own foolish greed and overly adventurous spirit.

Finding a way into the mortal realm offers great rewards in the Infernus. It is invariably how the mightiest warlords of the upper ranks accumulate power. There are various portals, places where the veil betwixt the worlds is thinned, but they are few, jealously guarded and perilous to navigate. Most of my kind who attempt passage fail, with destruction or permanent maiming their only reward. Still, I was young then, barely four centuries old by human reckoning, and youth married with curiosity is a dire combination. Reaching a portal required a journey equal to several human lifetimes, with much danger and pain along the way. But I was determined, obsessed you might say, and upon reaching the portal I felt a great sense of vindication, for through its shimmering curtain I beheld something demon kind lusts for above all else: the promise of human souls to capture.

It was all an illusion, of course, a farce crafted by Arkelion to lure me in. I knew my folly the moment I reached through the portal, the tempting vision transforming into the blank walls of bare metal. I tried to free myself, but his snare was too strong. It is a terrible feeling to be wrenched from one's world, my liege. To suffer the utter strangeness of another place, a prison where the only sensation is that allowed me by my captor. I perceived the world through his eyes. Heard what he heard, smelt what he smelt. Also, his thoughts...such a chaos they were. He was mad but also supremely focused in his purpose. 'Cease thine piteous bleating, cursed thing,' he told me. 'Rejoice, for thou hath been chosen.'

"Chosen for what?" Guyime asked.

That he didn't tell me. His mind, focused as it was, would often fade into a soporific mélange of regret and guilt. It was in these intervals of misery that I heard that name, a name I knew.

Kalthraxis, Guyime thought, keeping the sound from his lips. Lakorath had been insistent to the point of mania that they should avoid speaking this name out loud. Names had power, especially those borne by demon kind.

I understood that my captivity was connected to that name, Lakorath continued. *For I was not the first demon he had captured. I glimpsed Arkelion's memory of the day he trapped the Desecrator, seeking demonic power for his own ends, only to be made terribly aware of* his own monumental folly. Although, I didn't realise just who it was he had ensnared, merely sensing the terror engendered by his act.

"Desecrator?"

It's what we called the one I won't name, those who fought against his cause, that is. All demons vie for power, it is in our nature. So there is always war in the Infernus, but this was different. Amongst demons, alliance and betrayal are but two sides of the same coin. Concepts of loyalty are for mortals, except in the Desecrator's abnormal, twisted mind. Those who opposed him deserved only destruction. It is common for a demon to suffer, but rare for them to truly die, to suffer the end of all sensation and awareness, to be rent unto nothing. Yet the Desecrator's War saw the extinguishing of countless demons in pursuit of his lust for conquest.

"I take it you won? Given that you still exist."

After slaughter and discord ripped through the demon realm from end to end, yes, we won. With his last legion eviscerated, it was believed that the Desecrator had escaped to another plane rather than face the victors' wrath. No one could have suspected he had been lured into imprisonment in the mortal realm. Only when you spoke his name in that benighted keep did I realise we had suffered the same fate. With your map useless, the only clues we are likely to find as to the Desecrator's purpose lie amongst the ruins of Arkelion's island home in the midst of the Sorrow Sea.

"Ruins? So Arkelion is gone. Did you kill him?"

Would that I had. But no, that pleasure was denied me along with so much else. In truth, I know not how he perished in the end. My time in his clutches was brief and dreadfully confusing.

Eventually, after days or perhaps weeks, he recovered enough awareness to cast me away by means of some shifting spell. I found myself lying in a chilly, stinking bog for an appallingly tedious interval *until some passing simpleton trod on me. He offered only pathetic resistance to my will, and I soon compelled him to carry me back to Arkelion's island where I was determined to force the old bastard to send me home. Sadly, in the intervening centuries, he had contrived to perish, but not before weaving a final spell to confound me. It moves, you see, his resting place. Over the centuries it's been seen all over the Sorrow Sea, never lingering for more than a day. I exhausted the lifetimes of several bearers trying to reach it, never coming close enough even to catch the briefest glimpse. Eventually, I had the misfortune to fall into the hands of a strong-willed warrior woman from the southern wildlands and we spent decades together in the usual tide of conquest and tyranny. You remind me a good deal of her, come to think of it.*

"The island," Guyime persisted. "How do we reach it?"

Well, that's the turd in the stew bowl, my liege. I have no idea. The last time I made my way back here, the confounded place had begun to appear with far less frequency, as if the magic that bound it was fading. The entire story had slipped into legend, the Fable of the Spectral Isle, sought out only by the most determined or deluded souls intent on claiming the sorcerer's enchantments and treasure. None ever found it and I resigned myself to this occasionally diverting existence, until you came along, that is.

"This is where you guide me? In search of a phantom island that can't be found."

Where else is there to go, my liege, since your map can't be trusted? Besides, I've a feeling this is where we're supposed to be. The world is shifting like the block atop a crumbling pillar, and the tilt of it has brought us here.

Come the dawn, his companions gathered at the prow of the *Atheria's Grace* to watch the drizzle-clouded shades of an island chain resolve in the distance.

"The Crescent Isles," Orsena explained. "The port of Sovayir lies on the shore of the largest island. According to our esteemed captain, it's the last place that can lay claim to any semblance of civilisation before we come to the Sorrow Sea."

"A pirate den, I assume?" Anselm enquired. The young knight's features were drawn in a distasteful grimace as he surveyed the isles. He rested one hand on the hilt of his longsword, something Guyime saw him do with far more frequency than reach for the antique blade strapped across his back. In fact, he hadn't seen Anselm draw the Necromancer's Glaive since they departed the Northlands. From the way the knight's face twitched in repeated irritation, he divined that the voices within the blade were far from quiet.

"Some who find a berth in Sovayir are surely of that profession," Orsena conceded. "But I'm told they keep their criminal proclivities concealed whilst in port. The place is tacitly under the authority of the Allied Princes and the local magistrates are not sparing in their enforcement of merchant law."

The Ultria of House Carvaro paused to direct a cautious glance at Guyime. "My captain also avows a strong disinclination to sailing into the Sorrow Sea itself," she added. "Regardless of how generous I make his bonus."

"This ship is yours, is it not?" Guyime pointed out. "Would your father have tolerated such insolence?"

"No," Orsena said, a thin smile on her lips illustrating a tolerance of his occasional taunts. "He would have tied him to his own mast and had him flogged before the eyes of his sailors. But then,

I am not him. Nor was he, in truth, my father." She glanced over her shoulder at the sailors working the deck, each one seeing to their tasks with sullen diligence in between darting worried looks at the eastern horizon. "And the good captain merely reflects the mood of his crew. We can't sail a ship without hands."

"Sovayir is renowned as a busy port," Lexius put in. His eyes were brighter and larger than usual behind the lenses he wore, betraying a keenness to depart the *Atheria's Grace*. Guyime assumed Lexius found the bulk of the freighter and its copious holds an uncomfortable reminder of the slave hulks of his youth. "I'm sure finding a suitable vessel for hire won't be too difficult a task. Especially amongst those with a proven penchant for danger."

"As long as they've a destination to sail for," Lorweth said. The druid's mood had been the most soured by the lengthy voyage from Atheria, and his face betrayed a doleful contemplation of the islands looming through the chilly haze. "Which, as far as I can recall, your worship," he inclined his head to Guyime with sketchy obeisance, "you've yet to share with us in any fulsome regard."

Guyime's gaze slid to Seeker, the only member of their party yet to add voice to the discussion. The beast charmer stood in stern, inquisitive regard of the Crescent Isles, one hand idly stroking through Lissah's pelt. In response, the caracal arched her back and licked fangs in anticipation of setting paw upon the first land she had scented for weeks.

"We come in search of a place known as the Spectral Isle," Guyime said. "Where the Seven Swords were forged."

Seeker turned to regard him then, Lissah mimicking the movement to afford Guyime a customary hiss. She had come to tolerate the other members of this strange company, even displaying a certain affection for Orsena and Anselm. But, for Guyime, she only ever had hisses and scratching claws.

"We are guided to this island by the Cartographer's map?" Seeker asked, her tone lacking inflection although her gaze was sharp and steady.

"The Cartographer's map led us into the snare of Blackfyre Keep," Guyime reminded her. "So we can no longer trust it. We are compelled to look to our demons for guidance."

"*Your* demons," Seeker said, delivering a reminder of her own. "And I'd wager none of them care one whit for finding Ekiri."

"Ekiri's fate is bound up with the Seven Swords. Any knowledge we can glean as to their purpose brings us closer to her." Guyime paused before speaking on, slipping into the language common to the southern shore of the Second Sea. "I ask for your trust, sister."

Seeker's features tensed but she said no more, instead turning to resume her vigil of the isles.

It was Lexius who broke the subsequent silence, gripping the handle of the Kraken's Tooth with a tight fist. Guyime saw the glimmer of the blade at the edge of the scabbard as the being within made its feelings known. "My wife is content to follow this course, my lord," the scholar said. "With reservations."

"This one's happy to come along too," Orsena said, tapping a finger to the pommel of the Conjurer's Blade. "Not that I'd care if she wasn't. She does seem cheerfully optimistic that we're sailing to our doom, however."

Guyime turned to Anselm. The knight hadn't reached for his own cursed blade, though from the hunch of his shoulders and downcast features, Guyime could sense the struggle within the sword he bore. "It rages against us," Anselm murmured, raising his gaze to meet Guyime's. "But my other...companion placates it with promises of death." Anselm let out a dry, humourless laugh. "The only thing that seems to please it."

Guyime didn't envy Anselm his burden, for he alone amongst them was cursed to carry a blade inhabited by two disembodied souls. Even though one, the spirit of Sir Lorent Athil, was the most chivalrous knight and bravest soul to march under Guyime's long forsaken banner. Until now, he had imagined the two beings inhabiting the Necromancer's Glaive to be locked in an unending struggle for dominance. Now, it seemed Lorent had resorted to bargaining with the foul thing that shared his imprisonment.

Discomforted by the notion, Guyime shifted his gaze to Lorweth, raising an eyebrow and receiving a grudging nod in response.

"Very well," Guyime said. "From here on, there can be no more discussion. We must be united in our purpose, regardless of what lies in our path. I take your agreement this day as an oath sworn to unite the Seven Swords and return our companion's daughter to her. I'll make no threats nor utter dire promises, for I believe we are beyond that now. But make no mistake, we are henceforth bound to this course and only death will break our compact."

Chapter Two

THE COWED PORT

•————◦————•

The *Atheria's Grace* swept into the natural harbour of Sovayir on the evening tide, finding a dockside bare of all save a few cogs and fishing craft.

"Hiring another ship may not be so easy after all, your worship," Lorweth commented as the freighter's hull bumped the wharf and sailors hurried to shift the gangway into place.

Guyime was first off the ship, eyes narrowed as he scanned a quayside notable for an absence of the stevedores, merchants, and whores common to all ports. A few folk lingered at the edge of the dense mass of wood-built inns and storehouses fringing the docks. However, they afforded this strange group of newcomers only brief and wary glances before fading into the shadows.

"I offered the captain the equivalent of three years' bonuses to await our return," Orsena reported upon descending the gangway. "He replied with his resignation from future employment in House Carvaro and announced his intention to sail as far from here as possible as soon as the tide shifts. I pointed out that this made him a thief of my property, but he didn't care. Apparently, the sight of so empty a port was greatly disconcerting to him and his crew. He was full of whispers regarding dark humours on the air and ill winds carrying curses from the east." She let out a sigh and turned to regard the sailors already scrambling to ready the *Atheria's Grace* for departure. "Father always said sailors could only be counted on for two things: drunkenness and superstition."

"There must be a harbour master's office nearby," Guyime said. "We'll enquire there."

As was typical in most ports, the harbour master's domicile was a sturdily built fortress-in-miniature of stout stone walls, narrow windows, and a strong iron-braced door, the better to guard the taxes and berthing fees within. The crest of the Allied Princes was engraved into the lintel above the door, although Guyime found it significant that the usual banner was absent from the pole atop the roof. Some hard pounding on the door brought no response, although he did glimpse a flicker of light in one of the windows that bespoke a hastily snuffed candle.

"Open up!" Guyime shouted, pounding anew. "We're here on business!"

He kept up the barrage until he heard a snick and a small metal hatch slid aside to reveal a pair of fear-bright eyes. "Go away!" a voice instructed in a fierce whisper. "I'm honour bound not to consort with the Black Reaver's scum." There followed a pause during which Guyime heard the telltale gulp of a scared but resolute soul summoning courage. "Be off with you now! And know that I'm armed…and have many guards, and a particularly vicious dog not averse to human meat!"

With that, the hatch slammed closed with a loud clatter.

"Black Reaver?" Guyime enquired, turning to Lexius.

"A pirate king of dire repute said to haunt the Fifth Sea. The tales of him go back at least a generation, so I assumed he must have perished by now."

"Seems he's alive enough to scare the shite out of this bugger," Lorweth said, stepping forward to deliver a sound kick to the door. "We're not pirates, y'daft sod! Open up! We've coin to spend for information!"

Another shorter interval, then the hatch slid open, just a small amount this time. "Prove it!" Only one eye was visible now, still fearful, but also narrowed in wary greed.

"Sir," Orsena said, stepping up to the door and addressing the eye's owner with curt formality. "My name is Orsena Carvaro, Ultria of House Carvaro of Atheria. My house has many long established and lucrative contracts with the Allied Princes. Rest assured, should you fail to render assistance this instant, I shall be swift in communicating your appalling conduct to the Mercantile Court of Arbitration."

The eye narrowed further, betraying more concern than greed now. Apparently, the name of House Carvaro carried weight even here. Also, one glance at Orsena, a being crafted by magic to be the perfect example of her caste, would surely disabuse even the most foolish soul of the notion that she might be a pirate. A bout of rapid blinking told of feverish consideration before the eye disappeared and a reluctant but respectful voice muttered, "Forgive my caution, Ultria. But these are trying times."

There came a clattering and grinding of locks before the door swung open to reveal a small man with long, unkempt hair, his thin but pot-bellied form clad in shirt and trews that, judging by the stains and the stink, hadn't been changed for several days. He held a lantern in one hand and a dagger in the other. From the way he gripped the weapon, Guyime divined the lantern would pose more of a danger than the dagger.

"Well then," the harbour master said, moving back from the door and offering Orsena a short bow. "I s'pose you'd best come in."

"Your vicious dog, I take it?" Orsena asked upon following the harbour master into an office rich in untidy piles of paper, wherein the principal object of interest was a small, curly-haired dog lazing on a rug before the fireplace. It regarded the newcomers with yawning indifference until Seeker entered the room with Lissah perched across her shoulders. The caracal's customary hiss of greeting prompted the diminutive beast to let out a startled yelp before it scrambled for safety, not into the arms of its owner, but instead rushing to cower in the shadow of Orsena's cloak.

"It's all right, little one," the Ultria said, gathering up the whimpering creature. "She prefers more substantial prey."

"No guards either, I notice," Guyime said, turning to the harbour master, who was busying himself shuffling the copious paperwork covering his desk.

"Denied the proper protection that befits my office," the fellow replied with a peevish sniff, "I am forced to resort to subterfuge. Now then, Ultria." He procured a blank sheaf of parchment from somewhere within the pile of documents and sat, reaching for a pen. "Might I enquire as to the nature of your business in port?"

"I come seeking profit, sir," Orsena said, her attention mostly fixed on the small dog in her arms. His whimpering had abated now, replaced with an adoring cast to his large brown eyes and a desire to lick the face of this fascinating human. "Why else would I sail so far?"

"Of course." The harbour master dipped his pen and scribbled upon the parchment. "However, if I am to assist you, I shall require fulsome details…"

"We need a ship," Guyime cut in. Moving to the harbour master's desk, he extracted a gold Atherian talent from his purse and placed it before him, keeping his finger on the coin as he continued. "Preferably fast with a discreet captain who doesn't make unwarranted enquiry as to their passengers' business."

He saw a welter of questions behind the fellow's eyes as they flicked from the coin to the stern face of the hulking, grizzled man looming over him. It was when his gaze slipped to the handle of the Nameless Blade jutting over Guyime's shoulder that the questions withered into compliance.

"Would that I had ships to guide you to, sir," the harbour master said, tongue licking over dry lips. "But you have seen the state of the harbour. Near every craft that could sail the deep sea departed this port days ago."

"Why?" Guyime demanded, keeping his finger on the coin and inching a little closer.

"Because of this, of course." Trembling hands reached again into the piled documents, rummaged briefly, then emerged holding a small square of coarse parchment. It bore no writing, instead bearing the inexpertly rendered symbol of an eye.

"The warding eye," Lexius said, coming forward to take the parchment from the harbour master's unsteady hand.

"What is it?" Guyime asked.

"A pirate's mark from ages past. One I thought had fallen out of use. But not here, it seems. It's a warning, a marker of territory, you might say. Captains who receive one of these are placed on notice that their presence is no longer welcome in particular waters."

"You received this?" Guyime asked the harbour master.

"Not I. The captain of every ship in Sovayir awoke two weeks ago to find one nailed to their mainmast. The Black Reaver has decreed the *Axuntus Nuarem* his domain and will no longer tolerate competitors."

"This is a commercial port," Orsena said, brow furrowed. "Why would a pirate wish to scare off the source of his income?"

The harbour master blinked at her in momentary bafflement. "Why? Because it's back, my lady. Have you not heard?"

"What's back?" Guyime asked.

"The dread island, of course. It reappeared a month ago, much to the excitement of every pirate, cutthroat, and treasure hunter in the Fifth Sea. All the ne'er-do-wells in port sailed off to claim it right away, though I don't give much for their chances. If the storms and sundry vileness of the Sorrow Sea doesn't claim them, the Black Reaver certainly will. As I said, he will tolerate no competition and, according to rumour, has lusted all his life to claim the dread island."

"The dread island," Guyime repeated. "You mean the Spectral Isle?"

"It's been many a year since I heard it called that, but yes. It hadn't materialised in over thirty years, so long that some had begun to believe it just another seafarer's fable. It is, however, back. A ragged, storm-tossed cog returned with the tale

some weeks ago. The island reappeared in the very centre of the Sorrow Sea, apparently content to linger for more than a day this time."

Guyime felt the sword thrum with the signature vibration that reflected a certain smug superiority from its inhabitant. *And so, my liege,* Lakorath observed, voice rich in arch vindication, *the world tilts again.*

The narrow-hulled vessel sat at the very end of the docks, much of her structure lost to the dark as only a few lanterns glimmered on her rails. Despite the gloom, Guyime discerned this as a craft built for speed, a finely constructed clipper of sleek lines and three masts to catch every breath of wind upon the open sea. As they drew closer, he made out the figurehead jutting from the prow: a snarling serpent with a gaping maw baring dagger-like fangs. The vessel's name, etched in old Valkerin script on the bows, therefore came as scant surprise: the *Wandering Serpent.*

"Ask for Captain Shavalla," the harbour master said, coming to a halt well short of the ship's gangway. He stood with shoulders hunched and the collar of his coat pulled up, displaying a marked aversion to allowing anyone on board to glimpse his face.

"Not staying to make introductions, sir?" Orsena enquired.

"The captain and I are on…intemperate terms, Ultria. I feel your negotiations would be eased by my absence." He bowed and turned to go, pausing in irritation when Guyime asked a question.

"Why hasn't she sailed? Didn't they receive a warding eye like the others?"

"I've little doubt they did." The harbour master shot a resentful glance over his shoulder at the shaded bulk of the *Wandering Serpent*. "However, ever since she fetched up in these waters a year ago, Captain Shavalla has always followed her own course, regardless of the risks."

Bobbing his head, the fellow quickly disappeared into the misty gloom that invariably seemed to descend upon ports at night.

"Shall we see if the word of an Ultria carries as much weight with this headstrong captain?" Guyime asked Orsena, gesturing to the ship.

"Just flash a few talents from that hefty purse of yours, your ladyship," Lorweth advised. "But I'd recommend a tot of caution, too." The druid lowered his voice as they drew near the gangway. "I've a keen eye for a pirate ship. Gods know I've sailed on enough of them in my time, and I see one here." He nodded to the ship's hull, the lanterns' glow illuminating dark stains and deep, raking cuts to the timber. "Old scorching and the kind of scars that only come from battle. This is no merchantman."

Guyime felt the druid's judgement to be borne out by the reception they received from the two sailors stationed at the gangway. A man and woman of equally impressive proportions, they offered only scowls of dark promise in response to Orsena's polite greeting.

"We seek passage," Orsena continued, maintaining the bright smile that could often disarm even the most truculent of souls. Not so here.

"Piss off, y'snot nosed bizzum," the woman said, resting a meaningful hand on the hilt of her cutlass. Her tanned features, rich in tattoos which were in turn disfigured by several scars, began to crease into a snarl as she spoke on, "We ain't been asking for visitors nor passengers..."

Her words came to an abrupt halt at the sound of a loud, strident voice from the ship's deck. "Let them up, Corva! No need to be impolite to our guests!" The voice's unseen owner was female, speaking with a cadence and accent Guyime required a moment to place: the Ice Veldt of the far north.

Oh no, Lakorath groaned as Guyime followed Orsena up the gangway. *Please, not one of those myth-obsessed savages. Promise me you'll kill her if she starts reciting sagas, my liege. Even a demon can only endure so much torment.*

He stepped onto a silent deck, the crew of the *Wandering Serpent* pausing in their various tasks to stare at the newcomers. Guyime counted fifteen on the deck with another half dozen in the rigging above, all quiet and watchful. The sole exception was the tall woman striding to greet Orsena with an outstretched hand. The Ultria seemed momentarily confused by the gesture, being accustomed to receiving bows, but duly accepted the clasp with a gracious smile.

"Do I have the honour of meeting Captain Shavalla?" she asked.

"You do," the tall woman said, continuing to hold Orsena's hand as her gaze tracked the Ultria from head to toe. Guyime saw more than just careful appraisal in the woman's gaze, which wasn't unusual when strangers were confronted with so beauteous a personage. However, he recognized an additional depth of scrutiny and understanding in the way the captain's eyes lingered on Orsena's sword and utterly unblemished skin.

"Ultria Orsena Carvaro..." Orsena began only for the captain to release her hand and cut her off with a dismissive wave.

"Oh, I know all that." Abruptly, her gaze shifted to Guyime, eyes narrowing whilst her smile broadened. "I also know you are not the captain of this strange company. That would be this interesting fellow."

She strode towards him with an unhurried gait, boots sounding a steady and even beat upon the deck. Captain Shavalla clad herself in a mix of fine silks and hardy seagoing leather; her long hair, the colour of burnished copper rather than the golden hues typical to her homeland, was tied back from an angular face by a scarf of red satin; her skin was pale and smooth in defiance of the depredations wrought by years at sea. She wore a cutlass on the left side of her belt and a long-bladed dirk on the other, causing Guyime to recall the two-bladed fighting style of the Ice Veldt warriors he had encountered many years before.

"Did you know they call you the Kraken's Hand in Carthula?" she asked him. "What's left of it, that is. In Atheria, I heard an odd tale of statues brought to life to slaughter the Ultrii, only for them to be saved by a mysterious northern ruffian and his coterie of bizarre and disparate companions." Her smile widened to reveal a set of white teeth as she turned to regard the rest of their company, a careful, insightful gaze lingering on each one. "There's also a ballad or two about you journeying to the heart of the Execration to slay the Mad God himself, though even I find that one hard to credit, and I've seen many a wonder in my time."

She's doing it, Lakorath warned. *Telling stories. Just take her head then take her ship, my liege. You'll probably have to kill about half the crew to cow the rest into following orders. But that's a small price to spare us a saga.*

Turning back to Guyime, the captain laughed at the frowning suspicion on his brow. "Oh come now, old mate. You can't expect to blaze so bright a trail and not attract a reputation. Collecting interesting stories is part of my business. It's a poor captain who can't keep abreast of the changes in the world. You need to know which waters are troubled to steer a peaceful course. Good commerce requires it."

"Commerce?" Guyime asked, raising an eyebrow. "From the look of your ship, I'd say piracy was more your style."

Shavalla's smile dimmed a little. "Privateer, if you don't mind. I am between letters at present, but that would never compel me to stoop to wanton thievery and murder."

"Privateer?" Orsena asked.

"A pirate who has licence to pirate," Guyime explained. "When kingdoms go to war, they hand out letters of mark to ships willing to prey upon the trade of their enemies. Sea mercenaries, you might say."

"A fair description," the captain acceded. "One that brings us to the object of your visit, which is not hard to guess. You wish passage to the Spectral Isle, do you not?"

"We do," Guyime replied. "Our business there is our own."

"Nor would I dream of asking. But discretion, not to mention taking my beloved *Serpent* and crew into such perilous waters, requires an appropriate measure of compensation."

"I think you'll find this sufficient," Orsena said. Unhooking her purse from her belt, she tossed it to the captain.

Shavalla tugged the purse open to regard the contents. "Not enough," she sniffed, tossing the bundle of gold coins back to the Ultria. "The Sorrow Sea is a risky course at the best of times, and with the Black Reaver abroad, it's a veritable death trap. If I'm to risk ship, skin, and crew on a mad enterprise, I require more than coin, my lady. The wealth and reach of House Carvaro is famed, if not infamous. You are the undisputed head of a mercantile empire that stretches throughout the Five Seas, with a fleet operating in each one. Is that not correct?"

"It is," Orsena replied.

"Excellent. Then that is my price. Upon successful completion of this commission, you will assign to me all the ships in the Carvaro merchant fleet that sail the trade routes of the *Axuntus Nuarem*."

Orsena's unnaturally smooth brow betrayed a rare crease, her mouth tightening at the sheer effrontery of this proposal. However, Guyime also saw a grim resignation in her bearing. Like him, the Ultria's determination to see this mission through was unwavering, even in the face of such offensive greed. Meeting her eye, he shook his head to forestall her reply.

"Even if we were to agree to so outrageous a price," he said, "what guarantee do we have that you will reach the Spectral Isle before all the others currently racing towards it? As you say, the Black Reaver is abroad, and he already has a fleet of his own."

"He does," Shavalla agreed with a chuckle. "And dire will be our fate if his scum should happen upon us. But, if you wish a guarantee, old mate, I'll give you one: agree to my terms and I'll navigate the swiftest passage to the Spectral Isle, one no other captain in all the Five Seas could steer."

"And what surety do you offer should you fail in this boast?"

The question transformed the captain's mirth into a full-throated laugh. "My life, since failure will surely end it. And yours, of course, but I'd wager you and your friends are uncaring of such petty concerns."

Chapter Three

THE PRIVATEER'S GAMBIT

⟨•⟩————⟨•⟩————⟨•⟩

The walls of Captain Shavalla's cabin were decorated with what Guyime assumed to be an ancestral collection of various tribal accoutrements and weaponry typical of the Ice Veldt. Shields bearing faded woad sigils hung alongside helms that had been oiled and polished to stave off rust but were clearly of considerable age. Besides the wall hangings and the large silk-covered bed, the principal point of interest in the cabin came in the form of an ornate, rosewood map table. Upon leading them into the cabin, Shavalla briskly plucked a chart from the dozens resting in alcoves in the table's base and unfurled it on the baize top.

"The Sorrow Sea," she said. "In all its ugly glory."

Guyime recognised the chart as a true seafarer's tool, lacking the flourished borders, ornate calligraphy, and mythical sea beasts typical to decorative maps. Its original precise lines were augmented by a plethora of scribbled notes and amendments to the various depth soundings and arrows indicating currents. Guyime had some experience with sea charts, but most of the complexity was lost on him. He did, however, note the absence of most land masses to be found in this notorious stretch of ocean, the exception being a small cluster of islets a few hundred miles west of their current position.

"By all accounts, the Spectral Isle now sits here," Shavalla said, rapping her knuckles to the approximate centre of the map. "The northern approaches are guarded by the Graspers," she went on, tracing a finger to a series of dotted lines describing a chaotic course through a maze of currents. "Shallow waters rich in reefs that have a tendency to stick into a ship's hull and not let go, hence the name. It's also a shark's paradise. One of the few places you're still certain to catch a glimpse of the great hammerhead, usually just before it gobbles you up. Not shy about ramming a passing vessel, the hammerhead."

"Meaning this approach is ill advised, I take it," Orsena said. Her gaze was hard and steady across the table, Guyime sensing her chafed pride at the exorbitant bargain she was compelled to entertain.

"Only a fool sails the Graspers, my lady," Shavalla confirmed, shifting her finger once more. "The southward approaches are by far the best option. The Sorrow Sea is ever a treacherous bitch, even in the kindest seasons, so we can expect some of our competitors to find themselves embraced by the depths before this is over. But this is their only choice if they hope to reach the Spectral Isle."

"Then how could we possibly overtake them?" Guyime asked. "They're days ahead of us."

"Because we shall be taking the most direct route." Shavalla's finger moved to the cluster of islets he had noticed earlier. "Through the Ravenings."

"That sounds a mite worse than the Graspers to my ear," Lorweth said, peering at the chart with an evident lack of enthusiasm.

"It certainly is," Lexius said. Until now, he had maintained his habitual watchful silence, but mention of this particular name was enough to breach his reserve. His gaze was fixed on Shavalla rather than the map, Guyime discerning a certain accusatory glint behind the lenses. "The Ravenings crop up time and again in the most dire accounts of the Sorrow Sea," the scholar continued. "And in all of them, I never read of a ship ever escaping its clutches. It's a renowned graveyard of wrecks, a labyrinth of sheer rocks and narrow channels said to be infested with the ghosts of dead sailors, and more besides."

Shavalla afforded Lexius a respectful nod. "The scholar speaks true. Any captain with even the slightest modicum of sense knows to steer clear of the Ravenings. But I, thanks to peerless navigation and the stoutest heart, have mapped a way through."

Lorweth clicked his tongue as he squinted at the map. "I find my thoughts lingering upon the 'more besides' aspect of my learned friend's description."

"Sea beasts of unquenchable hunger," Lexius elaborated, his focus still on Shavalla. "They rise from the waves to swarm the decks of any ship foolish enough to invade their domain. So the stories have it."

"Mere legend, sir," Shavalla scoffed. "Sailed my course more times than I can count and never glimpsed a beast more interesting than a sea lion. This route is how I sustain myself in the lean months betwixt wars. No vessel can get a perishable cargo from one end of the Fifth Sea to the other faster than the

Wandering Serpent. Ask that cheating shit of a harbour master if you don't believe me. Besides," she paused to afford them a confident grin, "I'd worry more about the Black Reaver than any creature of dire imagination. If you want to beat him, this is the only way."

She's lying, Lakorath stated. From the stiff, hard-eyed bearing of his three sword-cursed companions, Guyime assumed the occupants of their blades were conveying a similar sentiment. *Not about all of it,* Lakorath went on. *There's truth mixed up in all the bluster, as is the way with practised deceivers. I'm fairly certain she does have the means of traversing the Ravenings, but isn't as sure of a safe passage as she pretends.*

"There's no such thing as a safe passage in this mission," Guyime said, addressing his words to Orsena, Lexius, and Anselm. They all took on the slightly hunched, tense aspect that told of communication with their swords. Anselm appeared the most discomforted, his jaw clenched and veins throbbing in his temples. Finally, hissing breath between clenched teeth, he straightened and nodded. Lexius was clearly reluctant, his own nod a slow gesture of resignation shorn of enthusiasm. Orsena's expression was only marginally less grave as she swallowed a sigh and turned to Shavalla.

"Your proposal is acceptable, Captain."

The *Wandering Serpent* sailed with the morning tide, Shavalla marshalling her crew to raise every sail so that by midday they plowed an eastward course at an impressive speed. For much of the day, the waters retained a calm that contrasted with the unruly swell they had endured aboard the *Atheria's Grace*. The clouds even consented to clear enough to allow a few rays of sunlight to paint a shimmer on the waves. Guyime began to wonder if the Sorrow Sea's reputation had been exaggerated, but, as the hour wore towards evening, the sky took on an ominous cast and the serpent figurehead soon heaved amidst constant white spray.

Guyime found Lexius at the prow, peering at the figurehead with keen inquisitiveness, apparently unconcerned by the occasional lashings of sea water assailing his slight form.

"Something of interest?" Guyime asked, coming to the scholar's side.

"The method and style of carving," Lexius replied. "Not often seen in the Five Seas, and this figurehead is plainly not original to this vessel."

"Our captain hails from the Ice Veldt," Guyime pointed out. "If I recall correctly, their sea-going war bands have a spiritual attachment to the figureheads decorating their longships. Their precise beliefs are obscure, but each band has its own god. So, even if a ship sinks beneath them, they'll risk all to save the figurehead."

"My knowledge of their customs is poor." Lexius's head dipped a little. Guyime had noted before that only ignorance occasioned shame in this man. "But Calandra recalls her father's dealings with some of their merchants. They put no stock in written contracts and insisted every deal be confirmed with a spoken oath, the breaking of which entailed dire consequences. We'll have to hope our captain is as diligent in keeping her word."

Guyime settled himself against the rail, leaning a little closer to the scholar, voice lowered. "I would know more about this oft-mentioned Black Reaver, since it seems likely we'll encounter him before this is over."

Lexius straightened a little, the words flowing from his lips with a precision that belied the fact that all the information came direct from his memory. "The earliest mention of the Black Reaver can be dated to just over three centuries ago. Then he was but one pirate with a single ship to his name, but made noteworthy by a predisposition towards viciousness and murder only matched by his avarice. In time, he acquired a fleet and a cluster of ports on the eastern shore of the Five Seas. These are lawless shanties where all the scum of the world are welcome, and from them he replenishes his crews amongst whom, it's said, he enjoys absolute loyalty. Much of the lurid detail regarding his career may be ascribed to the way legends accrue both horror and wonder with each telling. However, if even a fraction of it is true, he stands as the most feared corsair in all the Five Seas."

"Three centuries." Guyime frowned as a salient thought took hold. "Only magic can extend a mortal life so much."

"Quite true, my lord. But that presupposes the current Black Reaver is, in fact, the same man. Titles can be inherited or stolen, especially when they engender so much fear. There are, however, some tales describing the pirate king's employment of arcane rites: captives sacrificed to the more bloodthirsty sea gods in return for their dark blessing, and so on. Some stories ascribe the unreasoning fealty of his fleet to magical influence." There was a weight to the scholar's gaze that told Guyime they had both come to a similar conclusion.

"Any mention of him carrying a sword of ancient or unusual design?" Guyime asked. "One with a blade that glows, perhaps?"

"Not that I recall. There are some references to him wielding a weapon of direst power, but the details were vague."

Guyime ran a hand over his chin, gaze straying to the sea beyond the carved serpent where a bank of cloud had begun to spill a thick curtain of rain onto the grey-green waves. "If he is a sword bearer, it stands to reason he would seek out the source of his demon's imprisonment, either through choice or compulsion. It might well explain why he hasn't strayed from the Fifth Sea for so long, and his intolerance of competitors. Perhaps his demon has been awaiting the Spectral Isle's reappearance. Our mission here may have a two-fold purpose, my friend: divine Ekiri's intentions and secure another sword."

"A sword that will require a wielder," Lexius pointed out.

"Unless this Black Reaver can be persuaded to join us."

"Anselm and Orsena would surely object to sharing company with so vile a man. I'll confess to some amazement that they continue to tolerate me."

"A shared purpose can be a powerful thing, my lord." Lexius's eyes took on an unfocused cast that Guyime recognised as silent communication with his wife's spirit. "Calandra's sentiments are also reluctant to entertain inviting this Black Reaver to join our journey," the scholar reported after a brief interval.

"Then, I assume, she knows we have but one course should we encounter him?"

"She does. And neither of us will shirk our duty when the time comes."

"Killing him is one thing. Claiming his sword is another. No one can carry two demon-cursed blades. We learned that at Blackfyre Keep."

"Calandra has been pondering this conundrum during our journey. She believes there may be a spell that will contain the demon's influence and allow the sword to be carried, albeit with great care and constant reinforcement of the required magic."

"Meaning you would take on the burden, since she is weaving the spell. You would do this willingly?"

Lexius gripped the hilt of the Kraken's Tooth, his reply softly spoken but rich in sincerity. "I trust my wife's judgement, my lord, and her power."

The *Wandering Serpent* tracked an eastward course through variable seas for three days before the lookout in the crow's nest blew four long horn blasts. The weather had abated overnight, the sky dappled with only a light covering of cloud and the deck partially dried by the rising sun. Corva, the sturdy, tattoo-faced first mate, had charge of the morning watch. Under orders to maintain the sternest readiness, she was quick to order the large drum behind the helmsman's wheel beaten with the rapid strikes that summoned the crew to arms.

Guyime emerged from their billet in the hold to find the deck busy with sailors stringing bows and stacking arrows. Others pulled the tarps from mangonels and heaved them into place along both rails. Baskets of cotton-wrapped stone balls were placed alongside each device with buckets of pitch and lit torches held ready. He was impressed with the speed and efficiency of Shavalla's crew. The entire ship had been readied for battle within the space of a few moments.

"She's still afloat, Captain," Corva told Shavalla, handing her a spyglass and pointing to something less than a mile off the starboard bow. "Rain must've dampened her down overnight."

"Keep watch on all points," the captain replied, training the glass on a growing dark speck below the horizon. "Where there's one, there's like to be more."

Guyime moved to her side to watch the speck grow into the blackened, mast-less hull of a narrow-hulled freighter. Fire had consumed her upper works and much of her deck, stripping away the timbers to reveal the hold and cabins below. The wreck listed badly to port and Guyime saw water sloshing in her innards, meaning the sea would soon claim her. He couldn't make out the lettering on the scorched planking of the hull, but that didn't prevent Shavalla naming the stricken craft.

"The *Blue Orchid*," she murmured, lowering the spyglass. "One of the swiftest ships to ever be birthed by the Sallishan yards. Not as fast as the *Serpent*, mind you, but she'd have given us a good run."

"A pirate?" Guyime asked.

"Captain Freen was more attuned to the smuggling trade. There's a hefty bounty on his head in the Allied Ports on account of all the coin he cost their treasury over the years." Shavalla's lips formed a grim smile. "Seems no one will be claiming it now."

She raised her glass once again, tracking it across the horizon on both sides of the main mast. "This is not a good sign, old mate," she advised. "Means the Black Reaver has his dogs scouring the approaches to Sovayir, probably the Ravenings, too."

"Can you evade them?"

"As long as they're behind us. If they're ahead of us, however..." She shrugged. "Then we'll see if those swords you and your lot carry are just for show."

Chapter Four

THE FRACTIOUS SEA

—◆——◆——◆—

It had become Seeker's habit to spend most hours of daylight perched in the rigging. Shavalla had objected that the beast charmer, and her sharp-clawed caracal, were an obstacle to her crew's labour until Guyime assured her that Seeker assuredly possessed the keenest pair of eyes aboard. Her absence from his company may have been due to her essentially solitary disposition, but from the way she avoided his gaze, he divined a simmering anger beneath her expressionless vigil.

Oh, let her stew, my liege, Lakorath opined on the fifth day out from Sovayir when Guyime began his ascent of the mainmast. *Her perpetual pining for that treacherous whelp is wearying in the extreme.*

Ignoring the demon, Guyime made steady, if unhurried, progress to the upper reaches of the rigging. Upon navigating the various handholds to the crossbeam Seeker had chosen as her principal nest, he was obliged to dodge a slash from Lissah, narrowly missing the acquisition of a fresh scar to his nose.

"Has she ever made it clear why she hates me so?" he asked Seeker, clambering the last few feet to her side. Lissah afforded him a snarl before retreating to a higher position.

"You stink of death," Seeker replied with unvarnished promptness. "Decades of it seeped into your being so deep it can never wash. She hates you because she fears you."

Her voice was mostly bare of emotion, but he heard the resentment in it. Sighing, he heaved himself onto the crossbeam, settling his bulk close to the mainmast to avoid tilting the sail.

"The thing that commands Ekiri knows of our pursuit," he said. "If we continue to blindly follow the Cartographer's chart, we'll soon find ourselves blundering into another trap. This is our only course."

Seeker turned to him, her gaze fixed not upon his face but the sword on his back. "Did your demon tell you that? Can you truly trust the word of such a creature?"

Charming, Lakorath muttered.

"I trust its fear of the demon inhabiting the Crystal Dagger," Guyime replied. "To find it, and fight it, we need to know its ultimate goal. Knowledge will be our weapon, and the key to recovering Ekiri."

Seeker lowered her gaze, mouth hardening. The monochrome paint that once covered her features was long absent now, and he found he missed its facility for masking her emotions. Now he saw her anger, and her pain, all too clearly.

"Don't imagine I don't hear your doubt, Pilgrim," she told him. "You believe her lost, I know."

"We have travelled so far together, seen so much. In the space of months, we have uncovered mysteries and witnessed wonders I never saw in centuries of wandering this earth. I will not believe Ekiri is lost until the second we lose her, and I will strive with all I have to ensure that doesn't happen. In our company, we boast perhaps the most formidable collection of souls known to the Five Seas. If she can be saved, I doubt there are others more suited to the task."

"I wish it were simply a matter of trust." Seeker raised her face to the sky and he saw the tears she blinked away. "When first I lost Ekiri every night was a trial of dreams in which I chased her through endless deserts, always hearing her cries but never getting close enough to even glimpse her face. Even though they tormented me, drove me to the cusp of madness in truth, I cherished those dreams, Pilgrim, for I sensed that they bound us through the hidden channels of the world. Now..." She trailed off, drawing a deep breath. "Now those dreams have gone and I fear the cause. If she is not in my dreams, it means she has been fully claimed by the demon she carries, lost to me forever."

"You can't know that."

"No." She lowered her face, meeting his gaze, eyes still leaking moisture across her cheeks. "But I feel it. And I fear, Pilgrim, I fear the task that shall await me when we find her."

"It will never come to that."

She shook her head. "A promise you can't make."

"But I'll make it, nonetheless." He reached for her hand, grasping it tight. "Whatever it takes, whatever the cost. It will not come to that."

She returned his grip, just for a second, then released it. Turning away, she scanned the sea for a time until Guyime saw her stiffen into the predatory hunch he knew all too well.

"What is it?" he asked, his own eyes revealing only a blank stretch of ocean.

"What it always is," she replied with a note of weary resignation, leaping nimbly to her feet. "Another obstacle in our way.

For why would this endeavour be any different to all the others?" Standing, she reached up to thump a hand to the underside of the crow's nest. "Wake up! Look to the north and sound your horn! We have visitors!"

Fortunately, Shavalla opted to trust Seeker's eyes rather than those of her lookout who failed to spot the sail cresting the northern horizon for a full quarter spill of the hourglass after the beast charmer's warning. By then, the captain had summoned all hands to haul yet more canvas aloft whilst commanding various lines tightened and others loosened as she practised the mysterious art of the expert sailor. Soon the *Wandering Serpent* was cutting through the waves with a swiftness that made her prior efforts resemble a sedate walk.

Apparently satisfied with the set of her sails, Shavalla then strode to the stern to train her glass on the newcomer. Thanks to the *Serpent*'s superior speed, the ship was already well to their rear, Guyime noting the gouts of white water as it laboured to change course and maintain pursuit.

"She's one of the Black Reaver's, all right," the captain said, handing Guyime her spyglass. "See the flag?"

Raising the glass to his eye, Guyime eased the eyepiece back and forth until the upper rigging of the wallowing vessel came into focus. The flag trailed from her mainmast like a long, swirling bloodstain, dark red with a black motif of an eye in its centre. The ship itself was a substantial, wide-beamed warship with a sturdy, protruding prow designed for ramming.

"His flagship?" he asked, handing the glass back to Shavalla.

"No." She gave a rueful chuckle, eyes narrowing in appraisal of the pirate vessel. "His flagship is the *Shadow Claw* and she's a good deal bigger and faster than that fat-arsed tub. Judging by the state of their sails, they'll be far in our wake by nightfall."

Her satisfied grin turned to frowning annoyance when the lookout in the crow's nest let loose another series of blasts with his horn. "Clever bastards," Shavalla muttered, Guyime following her across the busy deck to the starboard rail. Short of the horizon, a second ship plowed a steady course directly into their path, hull angled as she knifed through the sea, her sails full. She was smaller than the vessel to their rear, but plainly a good deal faster, the red flag streaming back from her mast in a near straight line.

"You and yours best arm yourselves, old mate," Shavalla advised Guyime. "It's fighting time."

The opposing ship began assailing the *Wandering Serpent* with fireballs as soon as she hove within range. Mangonels along her rails cast a quartet of flaming projectiles in a high arc, each one leaving an ugly black trail across the sky. They plummeted into the sea a dozen yards short of the *Serpent*, birthing steaming water spouts and doing no damage. Instead of responding, Shavalla barked an order to her own mangonel crews to wait.

"No loosing until I can see their faces!" she called out before turning to the stocky sailor who had charge of the helm. "Five points to starboard to spoil their aim, if you please!"

Guyime gathered the others whilst the *Serpent* heaved in response to the angling of her rudder. The manoeuvre succeeded in frustrating the next volley of fireballs, although one delivered a glancing blow to the prow, leaving a lick of flame behind to be quickly extinguished by bucket-wielding crewmen.

"My lord?" Lexius asked, half-drawing the Kraken's Tooth and casting a meaningful glance at the swift vessel now heaving directly into the *Serpent*'s path. "One strike should suffice."

"Not yet," Guyime told him. "I'd rather keep our captain ignorant of our abilities a while longer. Besides," he jerked his head at the warship still labouring far off the *Serpent*'s stern, "I think your bolts would be best saved for them, should it prove necessary. Master druid," he turned to Lorweth, "any assistance you can provide in slowing it down would be welcome."

The wind weaver squinted at the pursuing vessel in critical appraisal. "She'll need to be a good deal closer, your worship. But I think I can keep her off us."

"Do so. If it looks as if they'll manage to board us, Master Lexius will do what is required. Ultria," he inclined his head at Orsena, "if you could linger here and see to their protection. Sir Anselm and I will deal with our most pressing issue."

"Leaving me behind?" Orsena enquired. Her tone held a note of humour but also reproach. "Do you doubt my sword skills, your highness?"

"Never, my lady. But I feel your particular brand of magic would attract too much notice. Best save it for more dire circumstance."

There was no argument from Anselm, the young knight having already drawn his longsword. The Necromancer's Glaive, however, remained firmly in its scabbard. "As you will it, sire," he said with a bow. Although he had avowed a pref-erence for addressing Guyime as 'captain', he did so with less frequency throughout the journey from the northlands. Instead, he increasingly employed the honorific used by Sir Lorent and the other members of the Ravager's twelve most trusted disciples. It was also apparent to Guyime that Anselm didn't realise he was doing so.

On the mid deck, Corva was busy organising a fighting party whilst Shavalla sent archers to scale the rigging. Guyime glanced up to check Seeker remained in place below the crow's nest. Raising a hand to gain her attention, he pointed to the ship now looming beyond the *Serpent's* bows. Her sails were trimmed and she bobbed in the swell, a dense cluster of armed men and women thronging her port rail. Smoke rose from blackened sections of her hull where Shavalla's mangonel crews had scored hits, yet none appeared to have inflicted vital damage. Arrows thrummed the air between both ships, one nearby sailor falling to the deck with a shaft embedded in his thigh and a stream of curses flowing from his lips.

Returning his gaze to Seeker, Guyime saw her calmly set an arrow to her bow, aim, draw and loose. Tracking the short arc of her shaft, he saw it claim an archer in the pirate vessel's rigging. Another two arrows followed in quick succession, each one sending a dark figure tumbling amidst the billowing sails.

"I think it would be best to conclude this business quickly," he told Anselm, leading him towards the prow.

"I heartily agree, sire," the knight replied. They crouched side-by-side in the shade of the figurehead whilst the enemy ship drew ever closer.

"Stand ready, you wonderful bastards!" Shavalla called out, drawing her cutlass as the fighting party drew up behind her, halberds and axes in every hand. She favoured Guyime with a wink as they waited for the *Serpent* to collide with the pirate's hull. "Glad to see you with us, old mate. I'd rather not waste deck space on a craven."

Beneath the humour and apparent keenness for battle, Guyime detected a careful judgement in her expression. *Wants to see what you're capable of,* Lakorath said. *This one's a mite too inquisitive for my liking, my liege.*

The swish and thud of thrown grappling hooks sounded across the *Serpent's* bows, accompanied by a chorus of hungry war cries from the pirates. A heartbeat later, the deck shuddered as the two ships collided, several sailors in the fighting party losing their footing only to be harangued back into ranks by Shavalla's lacerating tongue.

"Up, you wet-trousered bilge scum! Up and stand ready!"

The *Serpent* rebounded from the other vessel and a gout of sea water splashed the foredeck before the grappling ropes drew taut, the pirates heaving to draw them close enough for a boarding.

"I'm minded not to allow them the honour of the first strike," Guyime informed Anselm, reaching over his shoulder to draw the Nameless Blade. "Are you?"

"Certainly not, sire."

Guyime found the young knight's grin chilling in its resemblance to the long-dead man whose shade now inhabited the sword on his back. The shock of recognition was enough to keep Guyime momentarily rooted on the spot, allowing Anselm the opportunity to surge upright and launch himself over the prow. A desire to always be at the fore of every charge was another echo of Lorent's character.

Grunting in chagrin, Guyime rose and leapt onto the crest of the figurehead before hurling himself onto the pirate's deck.

The Nameless Blade pulsed a short but painfully bright glow an instant before his boots touched the planking, blinding those within sword reach. He scythed them down with two broad strokes as they staggered, their yells of alarm transformed into screams as limbs tumbled in a red rain.

Anselm was a dozen paces off to his right, fighting furiously amidst an encircling knot of pirates. Several had already fallen to the knight's longsword, but the others came at him with undaunted ferocity, cutlasses slashing. Starting forward, Guyime's path was immediately barred by a cluster of enemies. Like those assailing Anselm, they exhibited no trepidation, despite the slaughter just wreaked upon their crew mates.

Guyime had plentiful experience with pirates and the lurid, often garish manner in which they garbed themselves and tattooed their flesh. This mob was set apart by their apparent enthusiasm for self-mutilation. Every face featured numerous piercings, some deep enough to skewer bone as well as flesh. The bared muscles of their arms were rich in scars too elaborate to be solely the result of combat. Most significant of all were the eye-shaped sigils on their foreheads, branded into the flesh rather than tattooed. This, and the way they growled and snarled at him with a uniform pitch of bloodlust, forced Guyime to conclude these people had surrendered themselves to animalistic savagery.

Not so much surrendered as enmeshed, Lakorath commented as Guyime cut down the first pirate to lunge for him. *I sense magic here.*

"How so?" Guyime grunted, ducking under a slashing spear and laying open the belly of its owner.

It takes a powerful spell to enchant so many. That branding on their heads is the totem that binds them, instills an unwavering loyalty to whoever put it there.

With pirates closing in on all sides, Guyime gripped the Nameless Blade with both hands and spun. Flesh and steel parted as he described a bloody pirouette. Coming to a halt at the port rail, Guyime surveyed the trail of slain or maimed foes littering the deck. He noted that those not yet dead screamed and flailed like any other stricken enemy, the magically induced devotion to their pirate king seemingly overcome by mortal agony.

As is often the way, Lakorath mused. *The knowledge of impending death will banish all but the most potent spells.*

Spying another band of pirates mustering for a charge, Guyime swung his boot at a nearby bucket of pitch, upending its contents over the mangonel alongside and a good portion of the deck. Striking the sword to the iron bracing on the mangonel's arm, he scattered sparks across the pitch, birthing an instant blaze. Smoke soon wreathed the ship from stern to bows, rendering the crew into vague shadows, easily dispatched thanks to Lakorath chiming a warning whenever one came within reach.

Clashing steel and accompanying yells drew him to the aft deck, where he found Anselm heaving a wounded pirate over the rail. Despite having lost an eye and an arm, the fellow continued to flail and gnash at the knight even as he plummeted into the sea.

"A wounded adversary, sire," Anselm said as Guyime came to his side. The knight's features showed the distress of one wrestling with an innately chivalric nature. "But he wouldn't yield."

Guyime turned at the sound of something heavy thudding into the deck nearby, seeing the limp form of a pirate archer with one of Seeker's arrows embedded in his chest. Casting around, Guyime found no more living enemies, although arrows still arced down from the *Wandering Serpent*'s rigging. He huffed in satisfaction; the smoke served to conceal this victory, and he had a task to perform that would be best shielded from the eyes of Shavalla and her crew.

"We don't have long before this tub sinks," he told Anselm, moving to crouch beside the archer's corpse. "I would know more of our enemy."

A frown of deep reluctance tightened the knight's face, hands twitching and making no move to draw the blade on his back.

"I wouldn't ask this of you if it wasn't necessary," Guyime said. He hunched lower as a bundle of flaming tackle fell from the fiery mess of ropes and sails above. "And it must be done now."

Drawing a deep breath, Anselm reached for the handle of the Necromancer's Glaive, revealing the sickly green glow of the blade as he drew it free of the scabbard. "I'm not even sure how to command this thing," he said, crouching next to the pirate's corpse.

"The sword knows," Guyime assured him.

Tentatively, Anselm lowered the cursed blade to the corpse's chest, holding it in place whilst more blazing debris cascaded across the deck. "I don't think it's…" Anselm began, then stiffened as the glow of the Necromancer's Glaive flared into a pale emerald flame. The light bathed the corpse, Guyime seeing it seep into the wounds marring the flesh. The body shuddered and a thick wad of red gore erupted from its mouth. Anselm hissed wordless pain through clenched teeth, Guyime discerning the effort required to hold the sword in place in the sweat beading his tensed features.

"Ask it," the knight grunted, the sword trembling in his grasp.

Shifting closer, Guyime stared into the dead pirate's eyes, seeing the same green luminescence that had afflicted the dire wights at Blackfyre Keep. They had been creatures of mindless animus, driven to feast upon the flesh of the living without thought or memory. This one was different, its bloodied lips squirming and jaw working as it attempted to speak.

"You...torment me..." it said in a wet gurgle, red droplets spouting with every syllable. "Why?"

"Your master," Guyime replied. "The Black Reaver. Who is he?"

"Master?" A shrill approximation of a laugh spattered more blood from the corpse's mouth. "Slaver...I call him. Only now... in death...am I free of his chains."

"This." Guyime tapped a finger to the branding on the pirate's forehead. "This binds you?"

"Yes... His will was mine...for so many years."

"His true name. What is it?"

"I know...not. To me...he is only...slaver."

"Why does he hunger for the Spectral Isle? What does he hope to claim there?"

"What all men...of boundless greed...hope for." The glowing green eyes narrowed a fraction as the pirate focused his undead gaze upon Guyime. "I suspect...he wants...what you want, Ravager."

Guyime's hand clamped onto the corpse's skull. "How do you know that name?"

"He knows it…" The pirate bared crimson teeth in a smile. "So much he knows… So much the Morningstar reveals…"

"Morningstar? What is that?"

The light in the corpse's eyes flickered then, growing dim, its mouth slackening. "What is the Morningstar?" Guyime demanded, squeezing the pirate's skull. "Is it a demon-cursed blade?"

The green light guttered like a fading candle, then vanished, leaving Guyime to regard only the flaccid, empty visage of a recently slain man.

"Apologies, sire," Anselm said, raising the Necromancer's Glaive from the body. "It says this man's soul had lusted for death for many years. His will to die was stronger than the desire to cling to the illusion of life."

"We've learned enough." Guyime got to his feet, the deck swaying beneath his feet as the ship began to list to port. "Come on."

All but two of the grappling ropes attaching the *Serpent* to the pirate vessel had been cut away, drawn tight as the sea began to swamp the deck of the smaller ship. Guyime and Anselm made short work of scaling the ropes to the *Serpent*'s prow, where Captain Shavalla greeted them with loud admiration.

"Well, that's a sight to carry to the grave!" she called out to her crew, provoking an appreciative cheer. "Wish I'd had you pair with us during the Silk Wars," she added, clapping a hand to Guyime's shoulder. As before, he noted that beneath the hearty facade, her gaze held the same careful scrutiny, especially in the way it lingered on both his and Anselm's swords.

"The other two?" he asked.

"See for yourself." She turned, striding aft and beckoning for him to follow.

Lorweth sat on a rope coil near the stern anchor, back bowed and arms crossed, a familiar depth of fatigue showing on his greyed features. Beyond him the pursuing pirate vessel drifted in the gentle swell, the flames consuming her rigging sending a tall column of smoke into the sky.

"Quite the stroke of luck we've had today," Shavalla commented, shaking her head at the fiery spectacle. "First, two men alone manage to slaughter an entire crew and sink a ship, then a freak change in the weather robs their comrade of wind and makes them an easy target for our mangonels."

Guyime tracked the progress of the fire atop the warship, watching it consume the masts before spreading to the deck. Much of what transpired next was lost to the thickening pall of smoke, but he heard the screams clearly enough. Curiously, it was only when the inferno had covered both ships from bow to stern that the crews began to throw themselves overboard. Some were aflame and sank quickly, whilst others thrashed and yelled out desperate calls for assistance.

"It's custom to rescue survivors from a ship you've sunk," Shavalla commented. "Even pirates. They're usually willing to trade their allegiance at the drop of a cutlass, and I've lost three sailors to this scrap."

"Not these," Guyime assured her, turning away. "Leave them. The sharks have to eat too."

Chapter Five

THE TERROR
IN THE FOG

•)━━━━(•)━━━━(•

Contrary to expectations, the sea grew calmer the closer they drew to the famously treacherous Ravenings. Sails billowed sluggishly in the meagre breeze, pushing the *Wandering Serpent* through the mostly flat water at an unhurried pace. Shavalla avowed a surprising satisfaction with the parlous wind, remarking that it would make it easier to navigate her course. However, the thick bank of fog that descended the following morning caused Guyime to question the captain's apparent confidence.

"Just a spot of mist, old mate," she scoffed. "A true pilot could follow a plotted line blindfolded."

Guyime noted such certainty didn't prevent her from setting a double watch on the prow and ordering a cabin boy to sling the lead every half-turn of the glass to gauge their depth.

For much of the following day he saw nothing in the fog, the only sounds that of the crew working the sails or the creak of timber and cordage. For her part, Shavalla was content to perch herself on a tall-backed, leather chair on the mid-deck, calling out course changes to the helmsman whilst she puffed on a clay pipe.

"When do the Ravenings come into view?" Guyime asked her once the grey of the fog shifted into the dark hues of evening.

"About two hours ago," the captain replied. "We're sailing them now. You can tell by the churn. Currents grow swift in channels."

Moving to the rail, Guyime looked down upon a twisting, thickened swell.

"Depth twenty-eight feet!" the cabin boy cried out from the stern. "Bare rock beneath, Captain!"

"Good lad!" Shavalla called back, wafting her pipe in appreciation before turning to the helmsman. "Two points to port, if you please, Master Fynch."

"Two points to port, aye, Captain."

Despite the gloom, Guyime continued to peer into the obscuring mist, beset by a well-honed sense of threat, one echoed in Lakorath's judgement. *There's more here than bare rock, my liege,* the demon warned. *The stain of something...otherworldly.*

"Demonic?" Guyime asked in a soft whisper.

It has a whiff of the Infernus about it to be sure, but it's not of my kind. All I can say with certainty is that we shouldn't be here.

After another hour of searching the fog, his only reward a glimpse of a cliff-like silhouette soon lost to the encroaching dark, Guyime retired to the hold where his companions slept or sat in silent repose. Anselm lay on his bedroll in fitful slumber, features twitching and body jerking in response to the ugliness that beset his dreams. It had been this way since departing the Northlands, and Guyime found it a grievous sight. Whatever nightmarish memories afflicted the knight, Guyime doubted they were all his own.

Lorweth and Seeker were also asleep, though their rest was the unmoving stillness born of exertion. Lexius sat at a remove from the others, the Kraken's Tooth drawn and cradled in his lap. The scholar spoke in barely audible murmurs whilst the blade flickered in response.

"Do you ever envy them?" Orsena asked quietly as Guyime settled down onto his bedroll. She sat with her back propped to a beam, working a small knife into a block of wood. He had seen her whittle away at it occasionally during the voyage from Atheria, but since boarding the *Serpent,* it had become a far more frequent habit.

"Envy?" he asked.

"A love that survived even death." Orsena glanced over her shoulder at the softly speaking scholar, the thrumming glow of the Kraken's Tooth illuminating the face of a man lost in serene contentment. "And, thanks to the sword he carries, they will have centuries together." Frowning, she returned to her task with a sigh. "It sounds to me like something worth envying."

Guyime tensed as her words inevitably summoned memories of Loise, and the question of what price he would have paid to spend just one more moment in her company. "What is that?" he asked, looking for a distraction in her whittling.

"I find myself nagged by an artistic impulse recently," she said, her knife scraping another shaving from the block. "The consequence of carrying the Conjurer's Blade, I assume. And yet," she paused, raising the wooden block up to afford it a puzzled squint, "I remain largely ignorant of what this might become. It feels rather like I am a conduit for a creative force, one I can't really control. I wonder sometimes if Temesia felt that way when she worked. Something she surely confided in the real Orsena instead of her father's copy."

"That's how you see yourself? Merely a copy?"

She shrugged, smoothing a thumb over the unformed sculpture in her hand. "It's what I was made to be, is it not?"

"My father made me to be another version of him. An ambition I'm sure he ultimately considered the most terrible folly. We are never the people our parents wish us to be. And you, Ultria, are as real a person as I have ever encountered."

She gave no answer, but he saw her mouth curve in a smile before he unbuckled the Nameless Blade from his back and lay down, his hand still resting on the handle as the curse demanded. Closing his eyes, he attempted vainly to push his dead wife's face into the shadow as he sought the ever elusive grasp of sleep.

The rattle of the *Serpent's* anchor chain roused him sometime close to dawn, blinking at the dim light fringing the entrance to the hold. He could hear Shavalla's voice casting out a string of orders, followed by the rapid, overlapping drumbeat of the crew's feet upon the decking as they hurried to comply.

"Can't an honest man get some fecking sleep?" Lorweth groaned, sitting up to run a hand through his unruly hair.

"Honest?" Seeker enquired, rising with considerably more alacrity to reach for her boots.

"Since I met you, oh bloom of the desert," Lorweth returned, "I've had little option but to be as honest as a condemned man on hanging day."

"Why have we stopped?" Orsena wondered. Although she slept, largely, Guyime assumed, out of habit, he had become accustomed to the fact that her features appeared as perfect upon waking as at any other time.

"A very pertinent question," Guyime muttered, strapping on the Nameless Blade and making for the ladder.

Climbing onto the deck, he found the crew busy furling sails and stacking rope. The rattle and splash of the forward anchor made it plain the *Serpent* had been brought to as full a halt as her captain could orchestrate. He found her at the prow peering into the fog, one hand resting on the hilt of her dirk, the other playing over the wooden scales of the figurehead. The fog still lingered but had lost a good deal of its thickness, revealing a series of dark, monolithic silhouettes all around. They rose from the swift-flowing currents to imposing heights, yet Guyime heard none of the bird calls he expected. Such tall cliffs should have attracted colonies of gulls, puffins and others, yet all was silent save for the crew's labour and the slap of water upon the hull.

"Is there a problem?" he asked Shavalla, allowing an impatient curtness to colour his tone.

She spared him only a short glance before resuming her vigil. "Merely a pause to gain our bearings, old mate. We'll be on our way again soon."

"I recall a comment about true pilots and blindfolds," Guyime persisted. "Or was that just an idle boast?"

The captain's hand tightened on the pommel of her dirk, the first real expression of anger he had seen from her. "I have guided us this far, have I not?"

"This far and no further, apparently."

"The route will come to me. It always does."

"Come to you?" He stepped to her side, staring hard at her face. What he read in those guarded features made Lakorath's opinion redundant, but that didn't prevent the demon voicing it. *I told you she was lying, my liege.*

"You," Guyime grated, leaning closer to Shavalla, "have never been here before, have you?"

She sniffed, her posture shifting into rigid authority. "I'll remind you, this is my ship. Her course is only ever set by me. I have sailed us into the heart of a region few have ever lived to see, and I will sail us out again."

"And how, pray tell, will you do that?"

She turned to him then, eyes narrowing and knuckles growing white on the hilt of her dirk. Whether the confrontation would have escalated further would never be known, for at that very moment something swift and wet sprang from the sea to slap onto the rail between them.

Jerking back, his hand reaching instinctively for the Nameless Blade, Guyime grimaced at the sight of the pulsing, blistered thing clinging to the rail. Slime dripped from its glistening hide as it coiled about the timber, taking a firm hold, drawing tight as whatever it was attached to began to ascend the hull.

"What is that?" he demanded of Shavalla, receiving only a baffled, horrified glance in reply.

Hurrying to the prow with sword in hand, he looked down to behold the sight of a bulky shape dragging itself from the water. At first he took it for some manner of unfamiliar sea creature, a jumble of coiling tentacles rooted in a roughly oval body. But then it seemed to unfold, a small round object emerging from the central mass. Slime slipped from the protrusion as it revolved, three holes appearing in its surface. As the thing continued to drag itself towards him, the holes opened, revealing themselves as a wide mouth and two bright, staring eyes. Although the orifice was grotesque, an inverted sickle gaping wide to reveal rows of triangular teeth, it was the eyes that captured Guyime's attention. Instead of the blank orbs common to sea life, these were alive, knowing, and unmistakably human, for he had only ever seen such malice in a mortal soul.

Oh, Lakorath commented, the shared thought coloured by a dire sense of repugnant recognition. *So that's it.*

"That's what?" Guyime asked, then jerked back from the rail when, hissing, the human-eyed creature lashed a tentacle at him. The whipping limb missed him by inches, Guyime glimpsing sharp, thorn-like barbs emerging from the suckers on its underside as it flailed before his eyes. The Nameless Blade described a bright blue arc to slice through the appendage, birthing a chaotic fountain of black ichor that sent Shavalla reeling back.

Seeing the creature, hissing in both distress and rage now, drag itself the last few yards to the crest of the prow, Guyime lunged forward. The sword hacked through the tentacle latched to the rail in a cloud of ichor and shattered timber. Screeching now, the creature attempted to use its remaining limbs to gain purchase on the deck only for Guyime to cut them away with a few blazing sweeps of the sword. He completed the task by lopping the tottering monster's head from its twitching body, sending it tumbling back into the sea.

"What was that?" Guyime demanded.

"I have not the faintest idea," Shavalla replied, but his question hadn't been addressed to her.

Usually, Lakorath would feast on the blood of any creature slain by the Nameless Blade. Now, the creature's dark fluids slipped from the blue glowing steel instead of being absorbed. *Suffice to say, my liege,* Lakorath responded, voice laden with disgust, *this place is not what we imagined it to be, and it would be best if we departed with all alacrity.*

"Make sail!" Guyime snapped at Shavalla. The captain, however, failed to respond, staring in rapt fascination at the shimmering blade in Guyime's grasp. "Captain!" He gripped her shoulder, hard, causing her to blink in the face of his commanding snarl. "We have to leave. Now!"

"The course…" she began, only to fall silent when the air became filled with the sound of disturbed water. They both hurried to the prow once more, looking down to find the sea churning white as multiple bodies thrashed in a roiling multitude. Guyime saw more tentacles amongst the seething mass, claws too, and faces, all with the same bright, all-too-human eyes. From the accumulated roar of frothing water and the hisses of the monsters below, it was clear the *Serpent* was being assailed from all sides.

"All hands to arms!" Shavalla called out, her cutlass scraping free of its scabbard as she strode towards the helm. "Repel boarders!"

Chapter Six

THE RAVENINGS

 •———(•)———(•)

Within moments, the *Serpent*'s crew had begun to form a tight defensive knot around the mainmast. Fynch, the stocky helmsman, tarried too long to retrieve his axe and was jerked from his feet by a long tentacle that lashed over the port side to coil itself about his neck. Guyime severed the monstrous limb before it could drag its prize overboard, but it was too late to save Fynch. He lay still upon the planking, neck twisted at an impossible angle and eyes empty in death.

Seeing Lexius and the others emerge from the hold, Guyime rushed towards them, pausing to hack down a barnacle-covered figure that heaved itself over the port rail, lobster-like claws snapping and an obscenely long tongue darting from its mouth.

"Draw your blades," Guyime instructed, coming to his companions' side. "And don't staunch. The time for discretion is over."

Lexius was the first to respond, swiftly drawing the Kraken's Tooth and unleashing a bolt of lightning at the deformed mob now thronging the starboard bow. The air ripped with a cacophonous blast as the branching beam of pure energy shredded several creatures at once, a stench of roasted flesh and salt drifting across the deck.

Guyime staggered as Lorweth sent a whirlwind spiralling towards the stern, casting a dozen creatures up into the air to tumble away. To Guyime's left, Seeker's bowstring thrummed and he glimpsed a creature, seemingly mostly composed of coral, fall dead with her shaft skewered through its stony head.

"Get aloft," Guyime told her, jerking his head at the rigging. "You'll do more damage from there."

Seeker nodded, pausing to loose another shaft at a multi-limbed, crab-like monstrosity clambering over the port rail, before sprinting for the mainmast, Lissah bounding in her wake. Her arrow jutted from a gap in the crab creature's carapace, but it skittered towards them across the deck with undaunted eagerness, pincers snapping whilst emitting a hungry hiss. Before Anselm stepped forward to hack its forelegs away, Guyime fancied he saw two eyes gleaming in the dark recesses of the thing's shell.

Scanning the deck, Guyime saw the monstrous horde now cresting the deck on all sides. Shavalla's encircled crew battled the onslaught with impressive resolve, but in the space of seconds, he watched as two sailors were dragged down and butchered.

"Anselm!" he snapped, pointing his sword at the embattled crew. The knight glanced up in the act of dispatching the crab creature with a thrust of the Necromancer's Glaive, the cursed blade piercing its carapace with ease. Nodding in understanding, Anselm jerked the green glowing blade free and drew his longsword before charging to the sailors' aid, steel flashing.

"If I may, your highness."

Guyime turned at the touch of Orsena's hand on his arm. The Ultria had drawn the Conjurer's Blade, stained black with the blood of a slain abomination that lay twitching nearby. She pointed it towards the prow, grimacing in frustration whilst the blade flickered beneath the dark gore. "I need to get closer," she said.

"Lexius!" Guyime said, capturing the scholar's attention as he sent another bolt at the starboard rail. "Clear the path, if you would," Guyime requested, nodding at the stern. The intervening deck was thick with creatures, and it would take more time than they had to hack his way through them all.

Gripping the Kraken's Tooth in both hands, Lexius shifted his aim towards the *Serpent*'s bows. Guyime saw the strain in his face and the stagger of his feet, a reminder that, for all his abilities, the scholar remained a mortal man cursed to channel immense forces. However, there was no hesitation in Lexius's bearing when he steadied himself and unleashed another barrage of lightning. Instead of a brief burst of power, this was the sustained, unbridled sorcery of his wife's spirit, sweeping the crackling scythe of energy from port to starboard. Through the blinding haze, Guyime witnessed the disintegration of dozens of creatures, all rent to scraps in the space of a few heartbeats.

Lexius fell to his knees the moment the lightning faded, his slight form shuddering in pain and exhaustion. "I can…" he gasped, looking up at Guyime with an apologetic frown, "do no more, my lord."

"I think you've done enough," Guyime assured him before rushing across the charred, debris-strewn mess of the foredeck with Orsena close behind. Even before they reached the prow, more creatures had begun to boil from the sea, a forest of tentacles and claws poking over the smoking rails.

"Will this be enough?" Guyime asked as Orsena trained the Conjurer's Blade on the snarling wooden figurehead on the *Serpent*'s prow.

"It had better be," she replied. "For I believe we are sorely lacking in other options."

She concentrated her gaze upon the figurehead, features taking on a narrow, intense focus. In her grip, the Conjurer's Blade flared, the ichor covering it blasted away in a blaze of released energy. Unlike the swift-moving lightning birthed by the Kraken's Tooth, this sorcery moved with an almost languid grace, forming tendrils that snaked through the air to envelop the figurehead in a glowing matrix. The shimmering cage of light spread across the wooden serpent's scales, encircling its eyes, invading its mouth. Guyime heard Orsena emit a soft grunt of satisfaction before the last luminous tendril slipped from the tip of her blade.

"I think," she said, taking Guyime's hand, "we had best stand back, your highness."

He allowed himself to be drawn away, gaze still locked on the serpent, seeing the light that covered it seep into its timbers. As it did so, old, weathered wood became smooth, gleaming scales of emerald green with a rainbow shimmer. The spines along the figurehead's neck and back took on the shine of hardened steel, as did the fangs of its gaping maw. But what captured Guyime's notice most was the ruby that appeared in the figurehead's eye. It glowed with a bright, fiery energy, then flickered as the newborn creation of the Conjurer's Blade blinked at its first sight of the world.

Apparently ignorant of the powerful spell being wrought in their midst, the horde of monstrosities continued to haul themselves up the ship's sides, the air filled with a hungry chorus of hissing malice. One, a being of such utter foulness Guyime found its existence hard to comprehend, charged at them with blurring speed. Instead of one head, it had three, all dreadfully human. It scurried across the deck on many legs, some clawed, some ending in barnacle-covered feet, the mass of thrashing limbs on its back a thicket of talons and snapping pincers.

Guyime placed himself in front of Orsena, raising the Nameless Blade in readiness, yet before he could deliver a blow, a stream of red fire swept over the beast. The thing tumbled and wilted in a torrent of flame, its three heads shrieking in furious agony. Tracking the course of the fire stream, Guyime saw it emitted from the transformed figurehead's maw. The beast had torn itself from its union with the ship and reared amidst a mound of splintered timber. Snapping its mouth, it halted its flames then lunged for the roasted, three-headed creature, powerful forelimbs rending it apart. A dozen monsters threw themselves at the figurehead's back, only to be swatted into the sea with a few swipes of its tail.

Letting out a triumphant roar, Orsena's newest creation began a frenzied rampage, fire streaming from its mouth, limbs and tail rending and crushing. It scoured the starboard hull of enemies in the space of a minute. Upon reaching the stern, its progress was briefly delayed as it destroyed the throng of assailants that had become so dense their weight had begun to unbalance the ship. When it moved on to the port rail, Guyime saw the creatures there come to a halt. He saw no sign of fear or panic amongst them, just a momentary immobility before they all began to hurl themselves back into the sea.

"Something commands them," he said.

That it does, my liege, Lakorath assured him in grim agreement. *And I'd advise against indulging the delusion that it's done with us.*

Its enemies banished, the remade figurehead came bounding across the deck towards them, Shavalla's crew shrinking from it in justifiable terror. However, it paid the sailors no heed, instead lowering itself into a submissive crawl upon nearing Orsena. Placing its long, crocodilian head near her feet, its ruby eyes stared up at her in adoration.

"Perhaps your finest achievement to date, Ultria," Guyime said, affording Orsena a bow. "My compliments."

"Thank you." Orsena frowned as her creation emitted a puff of grey smoke from its maw, a long tongue emerging to caress its creator's feet. It let out a high-pitched sound Guyime soon recognised as a plaintive whine, one that only abated when Orsena crouched to run a hand over its snout.

"How long is it going to be with us?" Guyime asked.

Orsena glanced at the sword in her hand, which gave a slow, languid pulse of light by way of reply. "She doesn't know," she said. "Or care. It seems," she went on, a contented huff emerging from the beast at her feet as she rubbed the scales between its eyes, "I'll have to come up with a name for you, won't I?"

For a time, the *Serpent*'s crew stood around in dazed stupefaction at their own survival, gaping at the wreckage and corpses littering the ship. Patches of flame licked timber and rope in places whilst the monstrous bodies twitched and leaked ichor onto the planking.

Predictably, Shavalla was the first to recover her wits. "Stop staring, you grog-addled fucks!" she growled at her mesmerised crew. "Get these fires out! Corva, form a party to heave these ugly bastards over the side!"

"Aye, Captain!"

As he approached her, Guyime expected admonition, a resentful tirade regarding her passengers' failure to disclose their power before now. Instead, the expression he saw on her face was one of deep satisfaction, quickly replaced with a bland smile.

"You and your friends grow more interesting by the day, old mate."

"We have to leave," Guyime told her. "Now."

"A task I'll happily set myself to," she replied, before gesturing to the flaccid sails above. "But with no wind and no clear course to follow..."

"My lord," Lexius cut in, voice quiet but urgent. "The fog."

Shifting his gaze to the rails, Guyime saw the fog that had bedevilled their sojourn into the Ravenings had started to recede. Although he felt no shift in the air, the miasma swept back from the ship to speed across the water with unnatural speed.

"By the stars," Shavalla breathed, eyes wide as they beheld the revealed landmasses surrounding the *Serpent*. Instead of weathered rock fringed by kelp beds, each towering edifice was a grotesque mélange of wreckage and flotsam. Ships of both ancient and modern design were pressed into each other amidst a dense collection of sundered timber and maritime bric-a-brac. Masses of rope coiled like spilled entrails amongst the chaos, masts jutting from it like thorns, and upon them there stood more creatures.

"This must be centuries worth of wrecks," Lexius observed, eyes blinking in scholarly curiosity behind his lenses.

"And the crews," Guyime added. "Taken and twisted by whatever malignity lurks in this place."

From deep below the ship there came a sound then, a vast low-pitched rumble powerful enough to shake the *Serpent* down to every last timber and nail.

It appears we've made the mistake of commanding its full attention, Lakorath said. *Use of so much demonic magic will do that, I suppose.*

Guyime was about to enquire after the demon's meaning when the closest mound abruptly shifted. Debris and monsters fell from its flanks as it swayed and shivered, more rumblings sounding from below. The other mounds soon took on the same motion, the swirling current of the channels between them turning white with the movement.

Unless you would care to join this collection of mangled wretches, Lakaroth stated, Guyime sensing the rare glimmerings of fear in the demon's thoughts, *we need to depart this very instant.*

Guyime turned back to Shavalla, but the captain's attention was elsewhere, fixed upon a point beyond the port bow, hand clutching at her dirk in excitement. "There!" she said, pointing to the sea visible between two of the swaying wreck piles. "That's our course." A spasm of frustration tensed her face as she cast a glance at the stilled sails. "I'd give all for the smallest breeze just now."

"You should be careful with your bargains, Captain," Lorweth said, appearing at her side. The druid's face showed the customary fatigue that came from rigorous use of his power, but he stood with a straight-backed resolve that Guyime found reassuring.

"Got enough left, master druid?" he asked, receiving a weary smile in response.

"Just about, your worship. But when I'm done," he paused to step back from the mainmast, raising his arms to the rigging, "I'd ask that you not wake me for a day. Or, more likely, two."

The wind he conjured was gentle at first, quarter filling the mainsail, whilst Shavalla set about having the fore-and-aft anchors raised. By the time the *Serpent* was free of its shackles, all the central sails bulged with wind and she sped forward, knifing through the current towards the gap between the piled wrecks.

As the ship drew clear, the water swelled beneath her, creating a tall wave. Lifted onto its foaming crest, the *Serpent* tilted at an alarming angle. Sea water spilled over the rails, which served to banish the last patches of flame but also sent a pair of sailors over the side. Guyime was obliged to grab Lorweth about the waist to prevent him following suit, the druid still too preoccupied with his conjuration to notice. Shavalla had taken personal charge of the helm and let out a string of curses as she spun the wheel to and fro, somehow contriving to keep the *Serpent* atop the wave until, at last, it subsided and they found themselves in the open sea.

The interval of relief that followed was brief, the near hysterical laughter of the crew quickly swallowed by another sound. It might have been mistaken for thunder but for the deep, ululating notes that bespoke the product of a throat rather than weather. Beyond the *Serpent*'s stern the sea roiled as the wreck mounds continued to heave, shedding creatures and detritus all the while to reveal a surface not of rock, but dark, porous skin. The thunderous cry abruptly increased in volume as a great mass broke through the swell, its mountainous form rich in squirming tentacles, each a hundred yards long or more. Sea water flew like rain as it shook, Guyime discerning a face amongst the spume and coiling flesh. Two shadowed eyes and an inverted sickle of a mouth, a greatly enlarged mirror of the first creature he had killed.

The legends say it had a passion for remaking its victims into its own image, Lakorath said.

"You know this thing?" Guyime asked, watching the titanic head lower itself, a red glow appearing in the cavernous pits of its eyes as they fixed upon the *Serpent*.

I know of it, Lakorath responded. *A dark legendary horror, even in the Infernus. My liege, I present to you the Devourer of Souls.*

Chapter Seven

THE DEVOURER
OF SOULS

⟨•⟩————⟨•⟩————⟨•⟩

Lorweth collapsed after a heroic effort lasting nearly an hour, his summoned gale sufficing to keep the *Serpent* speeding ahead of the pursuing titan by a distance of a mile or more. However, when at last he slumped to the deck, eyes fluttering in exhaustion, the prevailing wind proved paltry in comparison.

"She's demanding I throw myself overboard," Orsena reported, wincing as she touched a hand to the hilt of the Conjurer's Blade. A bright, panicked glow flickered around the edges of the scabbard. After consigning a senseless Lorweth to blanketed oblivion in the hold, they gathered at the stern to watch the distant roiling draw inexorably closer. They could hear the vast creature's roar even at this distance, the evident rage and hunger of it reverberating across the waves to an ever louder pitch.

"Apparently she would prefer spending an unknowable span of centuries on the seabed to the prospect of being captured by this…" Orsena frowned, unable to arrive at a term equal to the horror that pursued them. "Beast," she finished, grimacing as the blade at her side flared yet brighter. "I must say, she has a surprisingly foul tongue when fear takes hold."

"Is it a demon?" Guyime asked, glancing over his shoulder at the handle of the Nameless Blade.

The Infernus is home to more than demons, Lakorath replied. *Beings that existed aeons before the first of my kind crawled from the birthing pits. The Devourer eats all, mortal or demonic, transforms them into mindless slaves in the caverns of its bowels and shits them out to serve its will. Long did it prowl the tides of the Sulphur Sea. Many demon lords sought to subdue it, make it a weapon in their endless wars. All failed, for its ferocity and hunger are boundless.*

"Then how does it come to be here?"

Arkelion's doing, I'd guess. The list of his crimes grows ever longer. Although powerful as he was, I never suspected him capable of such a feat.

"Can we fight it, sire?" Anselm asked. Guyime noted that no glow came from the Necromancer's Glaive on his back, and wondered if its inhabitants harboured any fear of death.

Sparing a glance at the sagging sails, Guyime sighed. "I doubt we'll have a choice before long. Lexius." He turned to the scholar. "Aim your bolts at its eyes. If we can blind it, we might have a chance..."

"All hands stand ready to heave to starboard!" Shavalla's cry interrupted his flow of orders, the captain spinning the wheel whilst her diminished crew hurried to reorient the sails. The steep tilt of the deck delayed Guyime's progress to the captain's side, by which time she had already spun the wheel back to midships and the *Serpent* had settled onto her new heading.

"We need to keep ahead of that thing," Guyime said.

Shavalla, her face tense with concentration, responded with a wordless nod towards the sea beyond the bows. Orsena's drake, as they had taken to calling it, had resumed its place amidst the splintered prow, obliging Guyime to peer through the smoke streaming from its nostrils before discerning the object of the captain's interest. Several miles to the south, the pale grey of the sky abruptly darkened into a bruise-coloured smudge above the horizon. Also, since they began their flight from the Devourer, the sea had acquired a definite choppiness. Feeling the first spot of rain on his cheek, Guyime turned back to Shavalla.

"A storm?"

"A big 'un, too, old mate." Her lips formed a grin, but the same hard focus lingered on her brow, hands engaged in constant, deft adjustments to the wheel. "I like storms. Always handy for getting lost in. That big bugger'll have a hard time finding us in there."

Guyime might have argued the wisdom of this course, if the only alternative hadn't been turning to fight the Infernus-spawned abomination looming ever larger to the west.

"Best get below," Shavalla advised. "And lash y'selves to something firm. You've never known a storm until you've felt the fury of a tempest conjured by the Sorrow Sea."

They were soon joined in the hold by the entire crew, save for Shavalla, who stayed aloft to steer the ship. The sailors busied themselves strapping every loose item into place, Guyime noting that they exhibited more fear now than they had during the battle with the Devourer's creatures. Their task complete, the sailors sat in quiet huddles, casting wide, dread-filled eyes at the deck above.

"I'd have thought this lot accustomed to storms," Lorweth commented. Roused from his torpor by the increasing howl of the gale beyond the hull, he still lay in his blankets. The price of his recent exertions showed in hollowed cheeks and a persistent cough whilst Lissah nuzzled his hand in a rare display of concern for a pack-mate.

"However bad it is," he went on after a short bout of coughing, "can't be worse than what we faced at the Spine, eh, your worship?"

Guyime glanced at the increasingly energetic sway of the lantern hanging above their heads, the first gust of savage winds sending a groan through the ship's myriad fissures. "By all accounts, master druid," he said, "the Sorrow Sea harbours yet more dire promise."

"Fret not, you land scrabblers," Corva stated, wandering over from the nearby huddle of sailors. Her disdain had a forced edge to it, contrasting with the fearful glances she darted at their swords. Although she had witnessed a fulsome demonstration of their power, Guyime liked her for refusing to be awed.

"I've sailed with the captain for nigh ten years," the first mate went on, raising her impressive arms to grasp the beam above. "Seen her steer a course through the worst weather this sea has to offer."

A wave struck the hull then, timber and nail vibrating with the impact as the lanterns rattled and shadows shifted throughout the hold. Guyime saw Corva wince and wondered if her trust in Shavalla was as firm as she claimed.

"So she steers through storms," he said. "And saw a way through the Ravenings when no other could, to a point at least. Have you ever wondered how she does it?"

The first mate's eyes narrowed, mouth flattening in a manner that made it plain she had in fact pondered this question. If she had ever arrived at an answer, however, she wasn't about to share it.

"Her folk are born to the sea," she said. "They can read the tides and the wind the way hunters read track and spoor."

Corva turned away before Guyime could probe further. "Get your coin out!" she instructed the huddled sailors, extracting a set of dice from her purse. "I'll not sit here with a thumb up my crack watching you miserable sots mope. Everyone bets on each throw, no begging off or I'll take a pitch-soaked rope to your back come the morn."

The following hours were an intermittently raucous travail as the sailors wagered with increasing abandon, their ribald taunts occasionally flaring into brawls. Such fractiousness would inevitably subside into fretful silence when a fresh wave tossed the ship, or a gust tipped her to an alarming angle. When the danger passed and the *Serpent* swung to a marginally less worrisome pitch, the dice and raised fists resumed.

Throughout it all, Orsena whittled away at her wooden block and Lexius communed with this wife's spirit. Anselm lay in typically fitful slumber, a feat Lorweth clearly envied but couldn't match. Seeker, never the keenest of sailors, sat with her legs crossed beneath her, eyes closed and back straight. Her lips moved in a silent recitation of a mantra, the purpose and meaning of which Guyime could only guess. The beast charmer was ever circumspect about her beliefs. He had never heard her mention a god, nor allude to the souls of ancestors. In truth, he had often felt her obsession with finding Ekiri to be so dominant that it left no room for any competing sentiment. Whatever the meaning of her cant, it apparently possessed sufficient compulsion for her not to betray the smallest reaction when the tallest wave yet slammed into the *Serpent's* port bow.

The deck heaved and the light flickered, then vanished as flailing lanterns shattered on the timbers. Sailors tumbled, scattering coin and dice, whilst thick curtains of sea water cascaded through the seams in the hatches. From above came the simultaneous boom and crash of both thunder and lightning. Corva's shout cut through the chorus of prayers, curses, and whimpers: "Put a cork on that wailing! You'd think you fuckers had never sailed before!"

More slamming waves followed, the fury of the storm rendering the first mate's attempts to restore order a fruitless exercise. For the next few moments all was darkness and fear, the gloom only dispelled when the main hatch was torn free by the wind. Lightning sheeted, casting a blue-white glow into the hold, revealing faces frozen in terror or despair. Curiously, even above the thunder and the shriek of the gale, Guyime's ears contrived to detect another sound. The pitch of it was lower than the storm's discordant howl, yet shot through with a note that mingled rage with plaintive frustration.

Great is the fury of a predator denied his prey, Lakorath observed as the cry of the Devourer faded into the cavalcade of noise. *It seems this gambit paid off, my liege. Now all you need do is survive this maelstrom. I'm bound to tell you that, in all my many years traversing the mortal realm, never have I witnessed a storm quite like this. The wind has a stink of sorcery to it, a particular scent I remember well.*

"Arkelion?" Guyime asked. "He conjured this, even though he's long dead?"

Many a spell lingers after the death of its weaver. His island has spent centuries shifting itself about the Sorrow Sea, after all. If you were a mighty sorcerer keen to discourage visitors, crafting an endless series of absurdly powerful storms would seem a good strategy.

More water washed through the hatch then, Corva resorting to liberal use of her fists to harangue the crew to sealing it with canvas. Most were too riven by fear to respond, even when punches bruised jaws or broke noses. Guyime and Orsena went to the first mate's assistance, hauling the canvas up the ladder so it could be nailed in place. As he ascended the steps, Guyime was obliged to extend his head above the deck. He looked upon a ship assailed from all sides by waves taller than her mainmast. A fresh bout of lightning revealed the sight of Captain Shavalla at the wheel, feet planted firmly and hands blurring as she angled it to and fro. It may have been some trickery wrought by the forking blaze of energy tracing through the roiling black clouds, but he was sure he saw her teeth bared in a bright, joyful smile.

The storm's fury began to abate before dawn, by which time even the whimpering or prayers of the most fearful sailors had faded into exhausted silence. Guyime climbed the ladder to the deck to find it a shambles of fallen sails and crossbeams. Scaling the steps to his side, Orsena let out a delighted laugh and rushed to the prow where her drake remained in place. The beast puffed twin columns of smoke from its nostrils in response to its creator's embrace, its tail moving in a manner that put Guyime in mind of a puppy enjoying its mistress's attention.

"I think I'll call you Tempest," Orsena said, running a hand over the drake's snout. "Suits you quite well, doesn't it? Yes it does."

Guyime was unsurprised to find Shavalla still at the wheel. Taking the pipe from her mouth, she raised it in greeting. "Quite the ride, eh, old mate," she said with a soft chuckle. "For a moment there, I thought this bitch sea finally had the better of me."

Despite her unflappable humour and evident vitality, he was struck by how youthful she appeared then. The violence of the storm had stripped away much of her accoutrements, her cutlass vanished but her dirk still dangled from her belt. Her hair was a tangled mass of damp red curls, her silken blouse torn ragged to reveal pale well-muscled flesh lacking scars. Corva claimed to have sailed with her for nearly a decade, but, if he hadn't known better, he would have doubted this young woman had spent more than a month at sea in her whole life.

"Do you, perhaps," he began, stepping over the intervening carpet of debris to come to her side, "have any notion of our current position?"

"Why yes, I do." She bit on her pipe stem, revealing white teeth in a broad smile as she inclined her head to starboard. Following her gaze, it took Guyime's less practiced eye a moment to discern a conical silhouette shimmering in the sun-lit haze of a clear morning.

"By my reckoning," Shavalla said, laughing again, "I'd put us about ten miles south of the Spectral Isle."

Chapter Eight

THE SPECTRAL ISLE

•———•———•

"**I**s that a mountain?" Lorweth wondered, squinting at the island slowly resolving out of the haze. The druid had recovered a good portion of his strength, though the stoop of his shoulders and hollowed eyes told of a lingering fatigue. Guyime would have preferred him fully recovered before they reached the Spectral Isle, given the uncertainty of what awaited them ashore. But, with the Devourer still hunting them and the Black Reaver drawing ever closer, they had not the leisure for delay. The druid's question had been prompted by the curious shape of the approaching island. It seemed to stand taller than it was broad, the narrow peak that dominated it composed of unusually sheer cliffs.

"No," Seeker replied, requiring no spyglass to discern details amongst the still vague silhouette rising from the becalmed sea. "It's a statue."

The wind this morning was so parlous, and the state of the *Serpent's* sails so ragged, that Shavalla ordered boats launched to tow them to the island. Guyime and the others lent their strength to the task, hauling oars for a full turn of the glass until the ship wallowed in a shallow anchorage off a crescent-shaped beach. Seeker's judgement had been starkly borne out when the isle came fully into view. The great figure of a bearded, robed man rose from a thick forest of trees to well over a hundred feet in height. The statue had been crafted from granite rather than marble, its surface dark and stained, but lacking the weathering and cracks Guyime would have expected from an ancient monument.

More sorcery, my liege, Lakorath informed him, his thoughts coloured by a bitter edge. *This was not the product of a thousand masons chiselling away for decades.*

"Arkelion," Guyime said, studying the grave, furrowed brow of the giant face looming above. The great effigy was posed with both hands raised, one holding what appeared to be a globe with the other positioned above it, fingers splayed as if frozen in the moment of conjuration.

I knew the old bastard thought a lot of himself, Lakorath said. *But didn't think his vanity extended to such absurd proportions.*

As the boat ground upon the beach, Guyime leapt clear to wade ashore, scanning the dense vegetation beyond the expanse of yellow sand. He saw only the sway of ferns and branches, plus a few birds flitting through the treetops.

"Anything?" he asked, turning to Seeker as she laboured through the surf. She had taken the precaution of nocking an arrow to her bow, but nothing in the forest prompted her to draw it. Instead, she stared hard at the trees, raising an expectant hand until a single bird rose from the mass of green. It was a colourful breed of red and blue plumage, resembling the parrots the merchants of the Third Sea liked to keep in cages, but closer in size to a falcon. It settled onto Seeker's outstretched arm with a squawk, blinking at her in contented fascination.

"Ancient songs and no memory of wingless two legs," Seeker said, smiling as she jerked her wrist, the bird taking to the sky in a blaze of colour. "If there's a threat here, it's not from beast or man."

"Still, we'd best be cautious." Guyime drew the Nameless Blade, Orsena, Lexius, and Anselm following suit with their own swords. Raising the blade, Guyime saw that it lacked the usual shimmer, its blue glow now constant and bright. "Any notion where we might look?" he asked the demon.

I recall a small palace, Lakorath replied. *Gardens, pools, fountains, and so on. Whether it still stands seems doubtful after so many years, but the ruins would seem a good place to start.*

Guyime cast a questioning glance at his sword-bearing companions, each of whom apparently had heard no more guidance from their own demons. "We'll head for the centre of the island," he said, starting forward. "Spread out from there."

"If I might enquire, old mate." Glancing back, Guyime saw Shavalla wading ashore, once again clad in her full finery. "Where exactly you're off to?" she finished, halting at the water's edge to rest her hands on her weapons.

"To get what we came for," Guyime replied. "Wait here and see to your ship's repair."

"You would deny me the prize so many have lusted for?" Shavalla's tone lacked anger, but he did see a new hardness to her gaze. Also, her crew had begun to form up at her back. They were suitably wary, but greed was always an antidote to fear.

"You seriously intend to fight us?" Orsena scoffed, shaking her head. "Having seen what we can do?"

"Got no desire to fight anyone, my beauteous friend," Shavalla replied. "But fair is fair. Me and mine have risked all, and lost good mates thanks to this venture."

"For which you were exorbitantly well paid." Orsena took a step towards the sailors, tone stiff with indignation. "And it has long been the tradition of my family to take a dim view of those who welch on a deal…"

"Ultria," Guyime cut in, shaking his head in response to her fierce glare.

Sighing, he turned his gaze upon Shavalla and the sailors. "You lot want treasure?" he asked, jerking his thumb at the forest. "Very well. Feel at liberty to go and find it. Any jewels, coins, pearls, or other frippery is yours to keep. I don't care. But, should any of you find a sword, or any other manner of weapon, I strongly advise that you don't touch it. If you do, you'll either be obliged to follow me for the rest of your days or I'll kill you and take it. The choice is yours."

Starting towards the forest, he gestured for the others to follow.

The sorcerer's palace proved easy to find, for it remained standing in the depths of the forest, albeit covered by a thick blanket of creeping vines. They snaked over every fountain, courtyard, and pillar, rendering what had surely been an elegant example of ancient architecture into an oddly shaped outgrowth of nature.

"The stone is still intact," Lexius observed, peering through a maze of vines at the wall beneath. "Barely a crack. It appears the forest claimed this place but couldn't consume it." He paused as the glowing blade of the Kraken's Tooth pulsed in his grip. "Calandra senses great power here. Diminished, but certainly not extinguished."

She's right about that, at least, Lakorath agreed in a subdued mutter. The bitterness that coloured his thoughts remained, but they were also now laced with trepidation.

"I assume Arkelion must have had a study," Guyime said. "Somewhere he worked his enchantments. Can you recall where it is?"

The sword thrummed, Guyime feeling a tug to the handle. He allowed it to guide his arm until it pointed to a thickly vined protrusion jutting from the palace's roof. *Sorcerers have a peculiar attachment to towers,* Lakorath said. *And Arkelion was no exception.*

"How do we get to it?" Orsena wondered, pushing at the thick barrier of vegetation covering an archway. Despite her inhuman strength, the mass of vines barely creaked under the pressure.

"I have often found, my lady," Anselm said, gently easing her aside and raising the Necromancer's Glaive, "that the simplest approach is usually the most effective."

That said, he brought the glowing sword down in a blinding flash, the vines parting before the cursed steel like silk at the touch of the dressmaker's shears. A few more slashes and the arch lay open, revealing an unlit hallway and curving staircase of gleaming marble. Whereas the palace's exterior had been allowed to succumb to the advance of nature, the interior remained completely untouched.

Anselm stepped into the gloom with typical boldness, Guyime close behind. Glancing over his shoulder, he cast a questioning glance at Seeker, receiving a shake of the head: still she sensed no threats.

Ascending the stairs, they passed through an upper storey rich in carpets, statuary and decorated urns. Here and there Guyime caught the gleam of silver and gold amongst the finery, something sure to please Shavalla and her crew. All was as pristine as if the inhabitants of this place had merely stepped from sight.

Continuing up the stairwell, they entered the tower itself. The shuttered windows cast slanting shadows over a circle of freestanding bookcases, each twelve feet high, their shelves crammed with leather-bound volumes. The arrangement of the bookcases resembled the stone circles to ancient gods Guyime had seen in the far north of his former kingdom. They surrounded a large circular table, its surface the matte black of slate, but completely flat and lacking any sign of imperfection. As he neared it, reaching out to trace a finger across the tabletop, the Nameless Blade gave a warning thrum.

Best if you don't, my liege, Lakorath cautioned. *It's not what it appears to be.*

"Then what it is?" Guyime enquired, only for Lexius to answer.

"A portal, my lord." The scholar crouched until his lenses were level with the table, eyes wide with fascination. "Long dormant, perhaps closed forever, but my wife feels the chaos that once raged beyond. This," his hand hovered over the unmarked surface, trembling a little, "is not stone. This is a substance not of this world. Something...alive, but best left sleeping."

"So this is how Arkelion pulled demons from the Infernus," Orsena said, her gaze slipping from the table to the bookcases.

"And I assume this is the lore he used to craft it." She gave a small laugh as the sound of Shavalla's pirates bled through from outside, voices raised in excitement. "If only they knew the true treasure here lies not in the shiny things they'll strip from this place, but in these pages. Many in the Exultia caste would beggar themselves to own just one volume of a library so ancient."

"Well they might," Guyime said, approaching the nearest bookcase. "For herein will lie the answer we seek." Extracting a book from the shelf, he was unsurprised to find the characters decorating its exterior completely unreadable, as were the pages within. "Lexius," he said, beckoning to the scholar.

"It appears to be a history of sorts," Lexius reported after a brief perusal of the book's contents. "Written in archaic triform. Some of the phrasing is so opaque I can't discern much meaning."

"No mention of demons?" Guyime asked. "The Infernus?"

Lexius leafed through more pages, his creased brow telling of scholarly interest but also frustration. "It seems to be a treatise on a series of wars fought so long ago many of the place names are completely unfamiliar. I find no obvious reference to sorcery, but a full study would require weeks, and this is just one book. Searching through this entire library would be the work of a year or more."

"We don't have a year," Seeker stated. "Ekiri doesn't have a year." Her gaze settled on Guyime, steady and demanding. "You promised answers, Pilgrim. I see none here."

"We must have patience," Orsena told her. "We have barely begun our search. We should separate, scour this palace..."

She fell abruptly silent when the sword in her hand let out a bright pulse of light, one mirrored by the other cursed swords.

Raising the Nameless Blade, Guyime felt a definite tug in the direction of the table. Extending the sword towards it, the steel glowed even brighter, taking on a rhythmic flare that intensified the closer it came to the black surface. Lexius, Anselm, and Orsena all followed his lead, their own swords flaring at the same tempo.

"What is this?" Guyime demanded of Lakorath.

The demon didn't respond with his usual alacrity. Instead, the voice in Guyime's mind was a stuttering, fading echo. *It's…* Lakorath grated, *…been waiting. Not…a portal. A…snare.*

Taking firmer hold of the Nameless Blade, Guyime tried to draw it back from the table, but it was as if the sword had suddenly become mired in rock. He renewed his efforts, and with a jolt, the handle slipped in his grasp. The sword still remained stuck in midair, pulsing light. It hadn't moved, but his hand had. For the first time in centuries, he had lost his grip on the Nameless Blade.

The shock of realisation froze him. He stared unblinking at his hand still clutching this sword, this demon-infested length of steel that had been his burden for so long. He knew without a shred of doubt that if he were to release his grip, he would be free. This was his reward from the sword's creator: bring the sword to the Spectral Isle and be freed from it.

His fingers twitched on the untarnished steel of the Nameless Blade's handle, but still he didn't open it. Forsake the sword and what then? Denied Lakorath's voice, Guyime doubted he would ever know the purpose of the Seven Swords. Surely Arkelion hadn't cast them out into the world simply to be returned here. Kalthraxis had a mission, and so did the sorcerer who once dwelt in this palace. Beneath the desire for answers, a darker, smaller sentiment lurked: simple fear. Without the sword Guyime, once the Ravager, later Pilgrim, and leader of this strange but wonderful company, would just be a very old soul in a body destined to age and wither as all bodies do.

Looking at his companions, he saw the same realisation playing out on their features. Lexius appeared distressed rather than hopeful, clamping both hands to the Kraken's Tooth and holding on with all his strength. Alone amongst them, he entertained no desire for release from his curse.

Anselm displayed a similar state of anguish, but for different reasons. The knight's sword arm shuddered, handsome features contorted in a manner that told of raging inner turmoil. His fingers flexed repeatedly on the handle of the Necromancer's Glaive, perhaps exhibiting the competing desires of those that inhabited it.

Orsena was the most calm, her perfect face drawn in stern calculation rather than indecision. Throughout their shared journey, Guyime had seen her exhibit mostly curiosity and occasional delight in the powers afforded by the Conjurer's Blade. Now he saw a more complex range of feeling in the unblinking stare she fixed upon her weapon. Although the Ultria was impossibly strong, perhaps even invulnerable, she was still the prisoner of a curse, one she hadn't chosen. It was the nature of all prisoners to desire freedom.

"I'll make no requests of you," Guyime said. "Nor judge any who choose to relinquish their blade. I have carried this cursed thing for so long I can barely remember how it felt to be free. But if I cast away that burden now, it has all been for nothing. Every mile walked, every agony suffered, every life taken, every battle fought. All meaningless. I came here for answers." He tightened his grip on the sword. "And I will not leave without them."

Lexius, his decision already made, gripped the Kraken's Tooth even tighter. Anselm gave a convulsive shudder, letting out a fierce grunt before clamping another hand to the handle of the Necromancer's Glaive. Turning to Orsena, Guyime found her expression still set in calculation. Her eyes flicked towards his and he saw a faint glimmering of shame before she looked away.

"No judgement," he told her. "The choice can only be yours."

"How do I know it's the right one?" she asked. "All of this may be just some diabolic scheme by a long dead sorcerer lost to the madness of his own ambition."

"You don't," Guyime conceded. "Neither do I. I do know that this is the only way we'll discover what this has all been for, whether it be good or ill."

Orsena's mouth hardened, the crease of her flawless brow deepening as she closed her eyes. "She wants me to hold on," she said, smoothing a thumb over the hilt of the Conjurer's Blade. "I feel her fear. I've also felt her malice, which is no small thing."

"In all the many years I have spent walking this earth, Ultria, I say in all honesty I have never encountered a soul more equal to malice than you."

The hard line of her mouth quirked a little. "I hadn't thought flattery one of the weapons in your armoury, your highness."

Guyime shrugged. "Any weapon is valuable, as long as it works."

Her half-grin blossomed into a full smile, one that vanished quickly as she too gripped her sword with both hands. "My choice," she said. "But know that won't save you from my ire should we soon find ourselves in the Infernus."

The decision appeared to act as a signal to whatever spell had captured the swords, their pulsing glow halting, then flaring yet brighter. The energy exuded by the four blades extended, merging, then subsiding into the black circle of the table. In response, the surface started to move, the alien substance that comprised it shifting like sand under a fierce wind. Shadows formed and coiled until they described a four-armed spiral, one that began to revolve, spinning ever faster as it grew in height. It ascended to form a whirling column some five feet tall, swelling and distorting in places. The column's movements were spasmodic, the shapes it produced vague and brief. Guyime fancied he saw a face amongst it, bearded and aged like the statue that loomed over this island, but it was gone in an instant.

The Nameless Blade shuddered in his grip and he heard Lakorath's voice as a dim, distant cry: *Not enough...* The twisting column collapsed with a suddenness that sent them reeling back from the table. The blades' glow died, all sensation of liberation vanished. Once again, the Nameless Blade sat in Guyime's hand with the irrefutable firmness he knew so well.

"What happened?" Seeker demanded. "What did you learn?"

"That we need more swords," Guyime replied, bitter disappointment adding a growl to his voice. "We only have four, and Arkelion crafted seven. I suspect we'll need them all to unlock this thing."

Actually, my liege, Lakorath said, his voice laced with a note of tired satisfaction. *I contrived to catch a glimpse of the old bastard's mind just now. Yes, he made seven swords but wasn't so foolish as to imagine they would all make it back here one day. We need but one more to summon him.*

"One more sword," Orsena said, the flicker of the Conjurer's Blade indicating her own demon had communicated the same message. "Where are we to find it? Ekiri carries the only other one we know of."

A new sound came to them then, a faint, pealing note reaching them through the shutters: the horn of the *Wandering Serpent*'s lookout. It paused, then repeated three times: the signal for an enemy vessel in sight. The Black Reaver had finally come to claim his prize.

"How fortunate then," Guyime said, "that we may have just been gifted with another."

Chapter Nine

THE SORCERER'S CURSE

•)————(•)————(•

By the time they reached the beach, the Black Reaver's flagship had weighed anchor in the shallow bay. The *Shadow Claw* dwarfed the *Wandering Serpent* by a considerable margin, a truly monstrous warship, her hull rich in iron spikes and a wicked steel ram jutting from her prow. Behind her, six more ships were busy trimming sail and dropping anchors, Guyime seeing boats being manhandled into place along their sides.

"I've fought long odds before," Shavalla commented, regarding the unfolding threat with her arms crossed and features set in a resigned grimace. "But none as long as this." She stood with her crew at the water's edge, making no move to fill the grounded boats and row for the *Serpent*. It would surely have been a pointless exercise. Even if they were to reach the ship, there was no hope of escaping so many foes.

"You could turn your coat," Guyime suggested. "A pirate king always needs more pirates."

"Privateer," she said, arching a reproachful brow at him. Her expression darkened once more as it returned to the

Shadow Claw. "Besides, he doesn't seem to be in a magnanimous mood at present."

Guyime followed the line of her gaze to the monster ship's prow, spying a hulking figure perched atop the steel ram. He was bare-chested and bronze of skin, a head of shaggy hair thrown back to emit a roar that could be heard even above the surf. Much of it was unintelligible, but Guyime discerned one word repeating amongst the raging babble: "MINE! MINE!"

As he roared, the figure whirled something, a spiked ball on a chain that glowed ever brighter the faster it spun. "The Morningstar," Guyime murmured.

"That very much resembles a demon-cursed weapon to me, my lord," Lexius said.

As if desirous of providing confirmation, the Black Reaver whipped the Morningstar, the blazing circle transforming into a fireball. It streaked across the waves to impact one of the *Serpent's* boats, rending it to smoking splinters. A member of Shavalla's crew fell with a shard of flaming wood speared through his torso. Three others collapsed, screaming and clutching wounds.

"MINE!" the hulking figure roared again before launching himself from the ram. He landed in the surf with a tall splash and began wading towards the beach whilst his crew cascaded down the flagship's flanks like hungry ants.

Guyime turned to Seeker and Lexius, nodding towards the horde now labouring its way to shore. "Kill as many as you can, then we'll withdraw to the palace. It'll be easier to wear them down from a position of strength..."

He trailed off upon noticing a familiar and worrying cast to Seeker's eye, the distant, preoccupied stare that bespoke use of her particular ability.

"What are you doing?" he said, gripping her arm.

"We need that weapon," she replied, tone flat, eyes unblinking. Beyond her, the treetops began to sway and shake with increasing animation. "One more, as you said."

"And we'll get it. As I promised."

"I tire of your promises, Pilgrim. This time, I will make sure." She shrugged off his hand and raised her arms, closing her eyes, body shuddering with the effort of summoning power. "I suggest," she hissed through gritted teeth, "that you duck."

"Down!" Guyime called out, he and the others throwing themselves flat onto the sand. He repeated the call to Shavalla and her crew as they stood frozen in baffled terror until a mighty collective squawk arose from the forest. The captain's eyes widened in realisation and she followed Guyime's example, yelling at her sailors to do the same.

A vast, rustling flutter came from the trees, drowning out the continuing roar of the Black Reaver. He had charged within thirty paces of the shoreline, the Morningstar blazing as he whirled it. As he drew close enough for him to make out his features, Guyime saw the deranged, scarred rictus of a man lost to madness for years. Neither this mad pirate king nor his followers showed any hesitation as they continued to splash towards the shore, even as the mass of enraged birds rose from the forest. A shadow descended as they swept across the beach, a maelstrom of screeching beaks and multi-coloured plumage. It would have been a pleasing spectacle if it hadn't transformed into a welter of red as Seeker's summoned flock tore into the Black Reaver's crew.

Charging pirates became thrashing, ill-defined shadows amongst the chaos. Blades slashed with desperate energy to hack the birds from the air, but there were always more. Beaks and claws rent flesh to a chorus of screams, human and bestial. The surf soon turned red as bodies began to wash onto the sands. Peering into the swirling frenzy, Guyime saw the birds had thickened around one figure in particular. Incredibly, the Black Reaver remained standing, still whirling the blazing ball of the Morningstar. Dozens of birds were blasted apart by the sorcerous weapon, but their mobbing of the pirate king continued undaunted.

Perceiving a change in the movements of the ravaging flock, Guyime saw Seeker wade into the crimson waves. The birds forged a path for her as she made steady, unhurried progress towards the beleaguered pirate king. Guyime needed no demonic insight to guess her intent.

Grunting a curse, he surged to his feet. "With me!" he called to his companions before charging in Seeker's wake. He waded only a few yards in before a pirate stumbled into his path. Both eyes had been torn from their sockets and his mouth streamed gore from a mutilated tongue. Birds perched on each of his shoulders to peck at what remained of his ears. Still, he tried to fight, swiping his cutlass to and fro in a maddened frenzy until the Nameless Blade laid open his chest and ended his torment.

Shoving the corpse aside, Guyime forged on, his progress continually impeded by streams of birds and stumbling, maimed pirates. Through the turmoil, he saw the birds mobbing the Black Reaver abruptly abandon their attacks as Seeker drew near. Freed of assailants, the hulking pirate king staggered, torso and face a bloody ruin of countless wounds, one eye dangling on his cheek from a thread of gristle. Still, perhaps due to the influence of the weapon he bore, he managed to repeat his war cry, thin and croaking though it was: "Mine!"

He sagged as Seeker drew closer, steam bubbling as his shredded arms allowed the Morningstar to slip beneath the waves. The beast charmer afforded him a grave nod before drawing her long-bladed hunting knife, making ready to slash a killing stroke to his neck. Before she could deliver the blow, the column of rising steam transformed into an explosive blast. The force of it sent Seeker reeling whilst the Black Reaver seemed to swell with renewed vigour. All vestige of his prior weakness vanished as he raised the Morningstar from the water, the spiked ball blazing brighter than ever.

"MINE!" he roared once more, whirling the weapon, angling the glowing arc of the ball at the flailing beast charmer. Yelling in wordless frustration, Guyime struggled on, knowing he wouldn't reach them in time. He could only gape in enraged horror as the Morningstar reached the apex of its swing.

Behind the Black Reaver, the water erupted once more as Shavalla reared up, her dirk raised high in her hand. A dirk, Guyime saw, that had a glowing red blade. Moving with the practised grace of an expert, Shavalla drove the dirk into the base of the pirate king's skull. He froze in the rigidity of suddenly inflicted death, the glowing red tip of the blade jutting from his mouth and the haft of the Morningstar slipping from his grasp.

"No!" Guyime shouted, seeing Seeker regain her footing and dive for the falling weapon. "Don't!"

She paid him no heed, disappearing below the blood-stained water to emerge seconds later with the Morningstar in hand. Knowing all too well the effects of first laying hands on a cursed blade, Guyime rushed to gather up Seeker before she collapsed. However, she remained standing, frowning at the weapon she held.

"Nothing," she said, looking up at Guyime, tears glimmering in her eyes. "There is nothing, Pilgrim." He saw that the Morningstar's haft, chain, and spiked warhead were engraved in a complex matrix of runes. They exuded a dim golden luminescence as Seeker's hands played over it, but the glow appeared weak compared to the flare of demon-inhabited steel.

She's right, my liege, Lakorath confirmed. *It's a magically infused device, to be sure. But it's never felt the touch of a demon.*

"But someone has," Guyime said, turning to regard Shavalla.

The captain returned his stare with a grin, jerking the dirk free of the Black Reaver's corpse as it bobbed in the swell. As she drew it clear, Guyime saw the pirate king's blood disappear into the glowing red dirk.

"Did you really think it a mere coincidence, old mate?" Shavalla asked. "The swiftest vessel in all the Fifth Sea and it just happens to be waiting to carry you to the Spectral Isle."

"You knew we were coming," Guyime stated.

"Of course I did." She twirled the dirk. "*She* told me. It's what she does when the mood takes her. Tells me how to find things I want, or need. And I've needed to find you for a very long time."

"For what?" Guyime sank into a fighting stance, holding the Nameless Blade ready. Shavalla, however, merely laughed.

"Same thing as you, my ancient friend," she said, the humour abruptly slipping from her face as she regarded the weapon in her hand. The sudden absence of anything but palpable hatred in her expression was jarring. "Freedom," she finished. "That's what you came here for, isn't it?" She looked up at him, enmity shifting to hope. Her voice cracked as she repeated her entreaty: "Isn't it?"

"I think this will have to wait," Orsena interrupted. Wading to Guyime's side, she pointed the Conjurer's Blade at the ships still disgorging the Black Reaver's pirate army.

At first, Guyime discerned a certain confusion in the way the many boats wallowed, oars flailing and crews babbling in consternation. But also, as comprehension spread, he saw an increasing sense of purpose. Their king and his malign influence may have perished here, but this was still the fabled Spectral Isle, renowned as the haven of many treasures, and these were still pirates.

"Back to the beach," he said, turning and labouring towards shore.

They were obliged to struggle through a tide of corpses, human and bird, before achieving the sands. By then, a new, dreadfully familiar sound began to overwhelm the pirates' excited chatter.

"Oh, feck it," Lorweth breathed as they turned to regard the fast approaching welter of displaced sea beyond the pirate fleet. "Clearly not a fellow to forsake a grudge, is he?"

The Devourer's scream was a vast, booming challenge as it hurtled towards the Spectral Isle, tentacles flailing, crescent mouth gaping, fire glowing in the depths of its pit-like eyes. Confronted with imminent calamity, the pirates succumbed to panic and desperation. Some attempted to row for their ships, only to see them rent to splinters by the Devourer's fury. Others cast themselves overboard and tried to swim for the island, all swiftly disappearing amidst a storm of white water as the titan of the Infernus began a feeding frenzy.

"The palace," Guyime said, running for the trees. "Arkelion summoned that thing. I'd wager he's the only one who knows how to banish it."

The Devourer's scream continued as they sprinted through the forest, growing ever louder in fury and hunger. By the time they reached the palace, it was near deafening.

"Draw your blade," Guyime instructed Shavalla upon entering the library, he and the others extending their swords towards the featureless table. She did as he bid, gasping in surprise as the dirk's steel flared and its unleashed sorcery began to merge with the other blades. Guyime watched the realisation on her face when she became aware that, if she chose, she could free herself of the demon she carried.

"Let it go," Guyime told her, the Devourer's scream now rattling the tower's shutters, "and you die. So will we, and so will your crew."

Her face tightened, angry recrimination blazing in her glare. "This isn't fair," she shouted above the Devourer's cry. "All I have dreamed of for so long is release from this thing."

"And you'll have it," Guyime promised. "Just not today. Freedom now means death for us all."

Closing her eyes tight, Shavalla revealed clenched teeth as she let out a grunt of sheer frustration and clamped both hands to the dirk's handle. In response, the table's surface once again began to shift, the same bearded face appearing amidst the rising vortex. This time, instead of fading, it grew more solid by the second until, within moments, they beheld a tall man of advanced years, regarding them with an expression of grave appraisal.

"Only five," he said, shaking his head. Although his voice was a sad echo, it cut through the Devourer's ongoing roar with unnatural ease. The resurrected spirit of Arkelion retained the same colouring and substance as the object from which he had been crafted, rendering his eyes into blank orbs. Yet Guyime still discerned a remarkable insight and intelligence as the long-dead sorcerer subjected each sword and bearer to a deep, searching scrutiny.

"The spy," he said, looking first at the Nameless Blade before shifting his gaze to Anselm and the Necromancer's Glaive. "The death master." Moving on to Orsena and the Conjurer's Blade, Guyime fancied he saw a fond curve to the old man's lips. "The crafter," he said before turning to Lexius and the Kraken's Tooth, whereupon his eyes narrowed. "Where is the soul drinker?" he asked. "The nehmavore? The essence within this blade is merely human."

"Driven out," Lexius replied. "By a more worthy soul."

"A terrible loss." The ghost of Arkelion lowered its head in sorrow. "Its power was crucial to our cause. As was the warlord."

"And what cause is that?" Guyime demanded.

Arkelion straightened, taking on an expression that told of a soul still suffering the torments of pride. "Such curtness," he said. "Have thee no manners?" He spoke on without waiting for an answer, angling his head as he peered closer. "Ah, there it is. The spirit of kingship abides in thine heart. A man accustomed to command and not easily swayed. Strange that the spy would attach itself to thee."

"I attached myself to it," Guyime replied. "Driven by the folly of revenge. Long has been the road that drew me here, and I will have an answer, sorcerer. What is the purpose of the Seven Swords?"

"Six," Arkelion corrected. "The seventh was forever beyond my control, and has its own purpose. To frustrate it, I created these." He gestured to the enclosing circle of blades. "Though, when the time came, I hoped all six would answer the summons. And of these five, one is corrupted. I fear our battle is lost before it begins."

"My wife's soul corrupts nothing!" Lexius stated. Not since that terrible moment beneath the bowels of Carthula, when Calandra took hold of the Kraken's Tooth, had Guyime seen such anger in the scholar. "She is the mightiest of sorcerers and the kindest of souls."

"Kindness?" Arkelion's laugh was thin but no less withering for it. "Thouest imagine that will avail thee in the struggle to come, little man?"

"We have no time for this!" Guyime broke in before Lexius could respond. "Another of your creations is about to rend this place to dust." He nodded to the shuttered window as the Devourer's cry shook it again.

"Oh, yes." Arkelion glanced at the window, a faintly sheepish frown creasing his brow. "I did wonder when she would fully awaken to the bounty offered by this world. I had hoped the scraps from the Sorrow Sea would keep her sated. But the scent of demonic sorcery was ever certain to rouse her."

"Why?" Orsena asked. "Why unleash something like that upon the mortal world?"

The sorcerer's sheepishness deepened into outright shame. "Because I could," he said with a helpless shrug. "Wisdom came later to me than it should have. But, terrible as the Devourer is, she is not the worst of my sins."

"Kalthraxis," Guyime said. "He was the first demon you summoned from the Infernus, wasn't he?"

"In truth, I'm not certain if I summoned him or he summoned me. All I know is that, when I beheld what I had drawn into our world, I knew myself to be the most vile criminal in all history. To look upon a being of such malign intellect is to behold the end of all things. For that is his object. I was the means by which the Desecrator of the Infernus gained entry to the mortal realm and in that moment, I divined his scheme and knew he had to be stopped.

"The Crystal Dagger was an arcane curio I kept for sentimental reasons, but was the only enchanted object to hand capable of containing his essence. But I had chosen poorly. By trapping him in the Crystal Dagger, I gifted him its ability to shift from place to place instantly. A spell requiring so much power it can only be done once a century. But once was enough. The dagger vanished the moment I imprisoned the Desecrator within its facets. Lost to me forever. But the stain of the demon's intent lingered upon my soul. My eternal crime, for which I now atone." He spread his arms, encompassing them. "In thee, my children."

"We're not your fucking children!" Shavalla spat. "We are your victims, old man. Have you any notion what it means to carry this thing? Family, friends, everything you know withering around you, making you an outcast, a wandering freak tormented by a demon's whims."

"Lesser crimes must be borne to rectify the greater sin," Arkelion replied. "Though, for what comfort it gives thee, know that I am sorry."

"The Desecrator's scheme," Guyime said. "What is it?"

"What all demons dream of," Arkelion said. "The conquest of the mortal realm. To this end, he seeks to open the Infernus Gate, if he can find it."

"The Infernus Gate?" Orsena asked, but it was Lexius who replied.

"A mythic portal between the Infernus and the mortal realm," the scholar said. "Constantly shifting, but unlike other fissures between the worlds, it is permanent. Legends say it was sealed by the demon lords themselves, for its very presence was a source of endless discord in the Infernus. Consequently, it can only be opened from this side."

Another roar from the Devourer, closer and louder now. The floor shook beneath Guyime's feet and from beyond the walls came the snapping rumble of something very large crashing through the forest.

"We have no more time," he told Arkelion. "Where do we find the Infernus Gate?"

"I know not," the sorcerer replied, a smile of apology bunching his beard. "I know only that thee must find the Desecrator and stop him. That has always been thy purpose. The closer he draws to his goal, the more those who carry the cursed blades will be drawn together to oppose him. This I wove into their very substance when I forged them. Only a demon can slay another demon, but to traverse this world, they required mortal bearers."

"How?" Guyime persisted as the entire palace began to tremble with the Devourer's approach. "How do we find him?"

Arkelion glanced at Shavalla. "Look to the navigator. For she was once his bride. Now." The sorcerer's spectre stiffened and turned to the north-facing window. "I have one last task to perform. Fare thee well, my children, for I can do no more."

"Wait!" Shavalla called as the sorcerer's spectre raised his arms. "If we do this, if we prevent the Infernus Gate from opening, will we be freed?"

Arkelion looked back at her, Guyime seeing unsuspected kindliness on his face. "The swords only exist as long as their purpose remains unfulfilled," he told her. "When thy task is done, the demons within will be released, and so will thee, my daughter." He turned back to the window, his last words to them a sorrowful mutter, "Should thou survive the Desecrator's wrath."

The window and the covering of vines beyond shattered as he extended his arms once more, Arkelion's dark form shooting through the opening in a blur. The collective glow of the five blades faded then, freeing them from the sorcerous vice. Rushing to the window, Guyime saw Arkelion as a dark streak across the sky. The Devourer was barely a hundred paces from the palace now, its vast form rearing amidst a swath of crushed forest. It paused in its advance when Arkelion sped towards it, spiralling around its head like a bothersome fly. Judging by the titan's ground-shaking roar and blossoming fire in its eyes, Guyime concluded it had recognised an old enemy.

Having fully captured its attention, Arkelion darted away, arcing through the sky towards the mighty statue. The Devourer's cry became a piercing, hate-filled screech as it laboured in pursuit, shredding trees and raising geysers of soil as it chased the sorcerer to the towering monument. Arkelion was barely visible now, a speck upon the globe poised in the statue's hand. The huge stone figure shuddered under the Devourer's first blow, a mighty arm slamming into its flank to send a matrix of cracks across the surface. It swayed and began to topple, but as it did so, the black dot of Arkelion merged with the stone sphere. The dark mote expanded quickly, covering the globe with its non-reflective substance.

This appeared to enrage the Devourer yet further, more blows from its arms shattering the statue's base. As it commenced its fall, however, the black globe suddenly emitted a glow so bright Guyime and the others were forced to shield their eyes. When he looked again, the partly-destroyed statue and the titan seemed to be moving through greatly thickened air. The Devourer's cry was no longer audible, its maw emitting a silent scream as it slowly writhed amidst a twisting cloud of rubble. The sphere's glow had dimmed, multi-coloured blossoms of energy swirling as it expanded, forming a vortex in the sky. Debris from the forest spiralled into the whirling nexus, along with what remained of the statue. The Devourer attempted to struggle free, tentacles and arms flailing in a slow, hopeless dance. But this last enchantment of the great sorcerer Calvius Arkelion was not to be denied.

The Devourer twisted and compressed under the weight of the vortex's sorcerous pull, mighty bones snapping and flesh ripping until it had become a near unrecognisable monstrosity. The spiralling energy drew the deformed titan into its dark centre, gathering up every last scrap of its being before, with a blaze brighter than the sun, it winked out of existence.

Chapter Ten

THE SCARLET COMPASS

◦)━━━━(◦)━━━━(◦

I t required the labour of several days to return the *Wandering Serpent* to anything resembling seaworthiness. Finding her still afloat in the aftermath of the Devourer's assault had been a remarkable turn of fortune. But, though her hull remained sound, her upper works were a mess of snapped beams and tangled rigging. Incredibly, a dozen or so members of the Black Reaver's fleet had survived, a bemused and mostly silent group all too keen to sign up with a new captain if it meant escape from this place of recent horrors. New masts had to be harvested from the forest, a task greatly hastened by use of the Nameless Blade and the most recent addition to their armoury.

The Morningstar's warhead glowed less brightly in Seeker's hands than it had when wielded by the Black Reaver. Still, it possessed enough power to shatter the broad base of a towering mahogany with a single blow. Guyime moved to the beast charmer's side as the crew began stripping branches and bark from the fallen trunk.

"Are you sure you want to keep it?" he asked. "All enchanted weapons pose a danger to the wielder, demon-cursed or not. And I sense an ill humour to this thing."

He perceived a defensive cast to her bearing as she took firmer hold of the Morningstar. "You and the others possess power I do not. This will balance the scale. And I will hold to anything that brings me even a step closer to Ekiri."

He watched her hands twitch on the Morningstar's haft, seeing the way the runes pulsed at her touch. "It gave the Black Reaver malign influence over his crew," he said. "Twisted his mind and theirs. I will not allow the same to happen to you."

"He was weak, as most men are." She turned away from him, gathering up the weapon's chain and walking off. "This thing is mine by right of battle, Pilgrim. You will leave its mastery to me."

Additional scouring of Arkelion's palace procured sufficient shiny items to placate Shavalla's remade crew, although they had been sternly dissuaded from venturing a hand towards any of the books from the sorcerer's library. The entire library was carefully transported to the *Serpent* and placed under Lexius's care.

A few hours later, Guyime found him ensconced within a veritable fortress of books, several already opened, his enlarged eyes flicking from page to page with eager animation. Knowledge was ever the scholar's principal passion, overshadowed only by the love he bore his wife.

"You recall Arkelion spoke of a warlord," Guyime said. "Presumably the demon inhabiting the final sword."

"My prior researches make no mention of a warlord's blade," Lexius responded, barely glancing up from a volume that appeared to consist entirely of garish and gruesome illustrations. "But if lore pertaining to such a demon resides in this library, then I'll find it. Though it may take me a good long while, my lord."

Tempest was another unexpected survivor of the carnage in the bay, clambering over the *Serpent*'s rails to greet Orsena, puffing smoke and nuzzling her feet, tail coiling all the while. The beast had been reluctant to leave the Ultria's side ever since. Guyime knew that when the time came to forsake this ship, Tempest would be another addition to their strange company, as would its captain.

He found her at the stern the night after their departure from the Spectral Isle, now a receding shadow far to the south. She acknowledged him with a brief glance before returning her regard to the dirk in her hand, the soft glow of the blade playing over her features.

"To anticipate your question," Shavalla said, a rueful smile curving her lips. "I found it in the far north, in an ice cave amongst the bones of a long-dead man. I wasn't even looking for it."

"What were you looking for?" Guyime asked.

She gave a brief chuckle, shaking her head. "The fabled silver crown of the last monarch to ever claim the title of the Ice King. Legend has it that whomsoever dons the crown shall rule the Veldt once more." She laughed again. "I was prone to such escapades in my youth. It's a depressingly familiar story: an old wizened charlatan sold me a map and, like a fool, I followed it. We sailed through berg-infested seas for months, finding nothing, my crew growing ever more fearful all the while. In my homeland, ships are not bought nor hired, they're won by blood. I was obliged to kill three challengers in a single day before the rest quietened down. I knew it wouldn't last. Sooner or later, they were going to pitch me over the side or feed me to a passing bear. So, when at last a stretch of land appeared, I was highly relieved, I can tell you. The charlatan's map was revealed as a fraud by the fact that it showed no land at this position. Still, I thought a little exploring would do the crew good."

She turned the glowing dirk over in her hand, a glimmer of the same hatred Guyime had seen before shining in her eyes. "And in a cave a dozen miles from shore, I found *her*. Just a nicely fashioned blade lying amongst the bones of its former owner. It was no silver crown, but it was something. So I picked it up."

Her arm tensed, hand gripping the dirk's handle with sudden fierceness. Guyime recognised this as a fruitless attempt to release a demon-cursed blade, one he had made many times himself.

Hissing a despairing laugh, Shavalla relaxed her grip. "The first time I heard her voice, it was like my mind had been bathed in poison. She is all spite. All dire designs and wicked schemes. She wanted me to kill my crew, make meat of them as we sailed ever deeper into the ice. When I wouldn't, she screamed commands at me for a full week until, lost to madness, I threw myself over the side. My sailors thought more of me than I imagined, for they fished me out, but I wasn't their captain anymore. Now I was just a madwoman they would abandon to the priests when we got home. Years I spent in the priests' care, a dull-eyed automaton, never speaking. My family came after a time and took me home. But, as more years passed and I stayed young whilst they grew old, they began to see in me a danger.

Whispers of curses and witchcraft spread throughout the village, and I knew I would soon find myself perched atop a pyre. I welcomed the flames.

"It was then that the demon's urgings changed, became quieter, more guileful. Apparently, she still saw use in me, even though I wouldn't bend to her will. 'Once you wanted treasure,' she said. 'Let me guide you to it.' I didn't trust her, how could I? But, at least she had stopped screaming. I took myself off one dark night and followed the course she set. Sure enough, a scant few miles to the south a merchant from long ago had buried a sack of silver coinage. Enough to buy passage to far away seas where, in time, she guided me to more trinkets, or ships to seize when I took on the privateer's trade. I began to call her the Scarlet Compass, for want of anything else, since she won't tell me her true name. Soon I bought my own ship, sailed her for a decade, then sold her and moved on. I've found it doesn't do for the ageless to linger in sight of the un-cursed."

Shavalla twirled the dirk, the glow flickering on her features. "Sometimes she fell silent for months. Sometimes she raged and hectored me to perform dreadful acts for her amusement. But mostly, she waited. I didn't know what for until she began insisting I take the *Serpent* to the Sorrow Sea. 'Someone is coming,' she told me. 'Someone we will both wish to meet.'" She paused, angling a glance at him. "At least she wasn't lying about that, eh?"

"Arkelion called her the Desecrator's bride," Guyime said. "Do you know what he meant?"

In response to his question, the glow of the Scarlet Compass shifted, becoming darker in hue. Shavalla paused her twirling to regard the dirk with a raised eyebrow. "You were married?"

she asked, voice edged in caustic amusement. "Who the fuck would have you?"

Another yet darker pulse of light, whatever thought the demon had shared causing Shavalla's face to tighten in anger.

Extraordinary, Lakorath observed, apparently genuinely impressed. *For two souls that detest each other with such passion to be entwined together for so long is truly remarkable.*

"Can you converse with this demon?" Guyime asked him.

Only to exchange expressions of mutual loathing, my liege. She hails from the upper ranks, you see. Talking to one such as me is considered very much beneath her.

"I need to know if she'll help or hinder this mission," Guyime told Shavalla. "Is she an ally of the one we seek?"

Shavalla grunted, the dirk's thrumming glow taking on an angry animation. "She finds the notion that she would assist the Desecrator in anything to be insulting," she said. "Once she was fated to be his queen, co-ruler of the Infernus, or so he promised. Like many a suitor, he lied, and she swore revenge. It was her quest for vengeance that enabled Arkelion to entrap her in this blade."

"Does she know where the Desecrator can be found? Can she lead us there?"

Shavalla frowned as the blade's glow settled into a more sedate hue. It betrayed a marginal flicker, Guyime divining a careful modulation in whatever thoughts it shared with its wielder.

"And how are we to trust you?" Shavalla asked, eventually. The blade flared bright once again, betraying offence suffered by a prideful soul. However, it quickly regained its former placidity. "Trust your hatred, eh?" Shavalla snorted. "Can't argue with that, since it's the only constant thing about you."

"The Desecrator?" Guyime prompted. "Will she guide us to him?"

"Better than that, old mate." Shavalla straightened, turning towards the prow. The Sorrow Sea was calmer now, the clouds thinned to allow the five stars of the Northern Crescent to shine bright above the horizon. "She promises to lead us to the Infernus Gate itself. For, she assures me, it's the one place on this earth we'll be certain to find her bastard husband. Though," Shavalla added with a hearty laugh, clapping a hand to Guyime's shoulder, "I should warn she also relishes the prospect of watching us all die when we do."